TIMBER GRAY

RONALD KELLY

Timber Gray walked around to the other side of the deadfall. Paul followed, holding the lantern ahead of him. As he glanced off down the pass they would be traveling the next day, Timber noticed a disturbance in the snow. "Bring the light closer," he told the boy. Slipping the thong off the hammer of his sidearm, he and Paul walked toward the swathe of churned snow.

The dark indentations were wolf tracks. From the vast number of them, it looked to be the pack he was after. The tracks were about half a day old. The snow had hardened, leaving a crust of solid ice around each print. Timber looked down the narrow channel of Burial Pass where the tracks disappeared into the night. The sudden realization that they were so near sent a chill down the wolfer's spine.

"Let's get on back to the wagon," he told the boy. They were turning to leave, when the yellow glow of the lamp caught a separate set of tracks apart from the others. "Wait just a minute," he said and knelt to examine them.

"Funny looking tracks," commented Paul.

He was right. They were strangely different from the others, although they were also made by a wolf. They were slightly larger, obviously those of the white-furred leader that Gray had seen the day he had sniped the pack from the rocky ridge. But the size was not the cause of his sudden interest. It was the right front paw print -- missing all the toes and half the foot -- that brought a smile of dawning revelation.

"Well, I'll be damned," he cursed softly. " If it ain't Old Cripplefoot."

Chapter One

Seth Adams fished a pouch of tobacco from his shirt pocket and began to roll himself a smoke. As he sprinkled the makings into the trough of the paper and licked the edge, his eyes never strayed from the desolate plain of southern Montana.

Cupping his hands against the bitter wind, he lit his cigarette. He drew the smoke into his lungs, then exhaled as he reined his bay gelding along a ridge that ran southwest toward the Wyoming border. Seth's horse stepped lively in the chill of early dawn. Its nostrils flared as a frigid northern wind hit their backtrail, then ebbed away into stillness.

Except for the wind and the easy progress of the horse and its rider, there was no movement whatsoever on the grassy expanse of the Whittaker ranch that morning. The plains were brown with frozen grass, the sky a violent gray with the threat of an approaching blizzard. Old snow from a couple of weeks ago lay in dirty patches beneath brush and leafless trees, untouched by what little warmth the sun could generate against the icy temperatures of late January.

Seth had worked for the Whittaker outfit for two years come March. He had traveled from his home in Amarillo, Texas to the cattle-rich lands of Wyoming and Montana when he was but a boy of sixteen. Seth had taken some ribbing and snide remarks from the bunkhouse veterans, but had soon proven himself a fair hand, especially with horses. He could ride and rope with the best of them, could handle a gun well, and wasn't too proud to be assigned the menial chores of the winter months like milking cows and gathering wood for the cook fire.

For the last few days the foreman, Bill Brighton, had him line riding along the Powder River. He and Charlie Piper had the job of covering a fifteen mile area, making sure the cattle didn't starve or freeze to death, the way the danged fool animals tended to do when the temperature dropped below freezing.

That was where Seth headed that morning, to look for Charlie. His partner had been out most of the night looking for a cow and her calf that had strayed from the herd. As of yet, Seth had seen nothing of Piper or the cattle.

He headed for a grassy meadow he had in mind, one with a watering hole and a few scattered trees that might provide shelter for a couple of lost cows. He couldn't understand it, though. Charlie would have surely checked the spot before any other and, if that was the case, should have herded the cow and her baby back into the fold by late last evening. But he hadn't. Charlie had been out all night. Seth had awakened with the dawn, expecting to find his buddy in the neighboring bunk. But it had never been slept in. And that didn't set right with the Texas-born cowhand.

Coming off the scrubby ridge, he urged his horse across a dry creekbed and up a small rise. On the other side was the pasture where the cows were most likely to have wandered. Seth grinned around the stub of his hand-rolled cigarette.

2

Maybe the calf had gotten bogged down in the waterhole. Perhaps he would crest the rise to find old Charlie knee-deep in cold mud, cussing and carrying the bawling calf back to the safety of its mama's udders. That would surely be something to fun poor Charlie about till spring roundup rolled around.

Seth's good-natured grin faded the moment he reached the top of the creekside rise. His cigarette dropped limply from his chapped lips and his lean face paled with a sick panic that he had never experienced before in his young life.

"God Almighty!" he rasped. His spurs needled the gelding's flanks, sending it down into the valley toward the scene of carnage that waited below.

The first thing that hit Seth was the blood. It seemed to paint the little clearing stark crimson, flecking the windswept grass and clouding the already muddy water of the drinking hole. Four bodies lay there on the frozen earth, bloodstained and torn, literally shred to pieces. The cow and her calf lay on one side of the watering hole. A saddled mare and the mutilated body of Charlie Piper lay near a spreading oak tree on the other.

The young cowhand swung down from his horse, which was siding nervously away from the ripened stench of new death. In the same easy movement, Seth pulled his Winchester from its boot. The .44-40 felt heavy and cold in his gloved hands as he walked toward the torn carcasses.

His eyes lingered on the cowhand and his horse for only a fleeting second, before the threat of rising bile forced his gaze elsewhere. Charlie had been killed in a way no man should be allowed to die. He had been set upon savagely and torn apart, his flesh and bone ripped asunder by the deadliness of flashing fangs. The horse and the two cows had been treated likewise, their inner flesh exposed, their entrails scattered away from them in the stiff grass of late January.

3

Overcoming the sickness of nausea and fear, Seth levered his rifle and fired into the cold, gray sky. The report thundered across the Montana flatland, followed closely by another. After the last shot died in his ears, there was only the emptiness of silence. A silence that had followed the awful sounds of screaming and the deadly snaps and snarls of a murderous pack only a few twilight hours ago.

Seth Adams backed away and sat on a boulder at the edge of the meadow, wrapped in the warm confines of a thick, woolen coat, but shivering cold never the less. His hands clutched the Winchester until his knuckles whitened and his frightened eyes looked to the south, watching for darting gray forms which had long since escaped across the plains.

Soon, the drumming of hooves and the excited shouts of Whittaker hands reached his reddened ears. But he did not move from his spot, nor pull his vigilant gaze from the horizon. He could only sit there and remember something his pa, an old cattleman himself, had told him the day he left Texas.

"Son," the old man had warned, "you'll be riding into some hard country now. A land where cattle is king and where everything else; weather, man, or beast is out to bring it down. There are four things you'd best keep watch for. Things that could be the death of you in the flickering of an eye."

He remembered the old man's face as he counted off the hazards, remembered the weathered features of a man who had seen his share of all four. "Blizzard, injuns, rustlers, and, perhaps the most dangerous of them all…"

Wolves.

Chapter Two

Louis B. Whittaker was known throughout the Montana territory as one of the richest of cattle barons. Some said he owned over fifty thousand head of prime beef on his fifty mile spread, which was nestled between the Yellowstone and Powder Rivers, just south of Miles City.

But despite the rumor of him being a pompous, money-hungry man, Whittaker considered himself as "just plain folks". So did the men who worked for him. They knew they could come to this quiet, one-armed man and unburden their troubles any hour of the day or night. So it wasn't unusual that a small group of Whittaker's hands stood expectantly in the cattle baron's parlor on that blustery January morn, their hats in their hands and their thoughts lingering angrily and uncomfortably on the awful fate of their friend, Charlie Piper.

Whittaker stood at a tall, curtained window of his sitting room. He stared solemnly through the frosty panes as two men lifted the cowhand's body off a horse and laid it gently on a wagon bed. The blanket that Piper had been wrapped in was stained with blood. The cattleman pulled his intense blue eyes from the scene outside and centered his attention on the four who stood nervously near the parlor doorway.

"It was those confounded wolves again!" he said, but it came out more as a curse than a question.

"Yes, sir," replied his foreman, Bill Brighton, a large, bearded man in a buffalo skin coat and shapeless gray hat. "It looked to be the very same pack that killed those seven head last week." Two men, Joe Boyce and Ralph Henry, stood to the foreman's left, while Seth Adams, looking pale and shaken, stood to his right, still holding the Winchester in his hands.

Louis Whittaker paced the carpeted floor of his parlor. He was a tall, silver-haired man with sharp features and piercing ice-blue eyes beneath heavy brows. He was a devout Christian and a gentleman born of the Old South. He had led a brigade of Wheeler's cavalry during the War Between the States. It was during one such charge that he had lost his left arm. A cannonball at Stones River had severed his arm cleanly at the elbow as he led his Confederate riders down upon an unsuspecting group of Yankee infantry. The wound would have killed most men or subjected others to the life of a hopeless cripple. But not Louis B. Whittaker. He had traveled westward and forged a new life from a hard and brutal land. Starting with only a few head of cattle, he had built a vast empire in the brief span of only fifteen years.

On that day, however, the old man's thoughts lay on things other than success and good fortune. All that he could think about was unfortunate Charlie Piper, set upon by a monstrous pack of savage timber wolves; wolves that had killed his cattle for over a month now. If the reports were correct, the pack's number was near fifty; larger than any wolf pack that had ever crossed the Montana territory, or the territories of Wyoming and the Dakotas combined. No one knew exactly where the beasts were heading, but Whittaker knew where they had been.

They had crossed his land, staying to the forests until an insatiable hunger drove them onto the open plains to kill.

"Let us go after 'em, sir," urged Brighton. "I'll round up some of the boys and we'll hunt down the varmints that killed poor Charlie."

"You know I can't do that, Bill," the cattleman replied. "We're shorthanded as it is. We just don't have the manpower to spare." After the summer drive, most of his hands were working jobs in town or grub-lining. If word got out that half his winter hands were out wolf hunting, there was bound to be some rustling.

An awkward silence elapsed for a time, then one of the hands stepped forward and cleared his throat. "Mr. Whittaker?"

"Yes, Joe?"

"I heard tell there's a wolfer in Miles City. The one they call Timber Gray."

Whittaker's eyes settled on Joe Boyce, as did those of Brighton and the other two cowboys. The cattle baron's gaze twinkled with a new hope. "Timber Gray," he whispered.

The name was not unfamiliar to any of them. Most men west of the Mississippi had heard of the man who hunted dangerous game for the right bounty. Be it grizzly, mountain lion, or entire packs of wolves; the man called Timber Gray was the one to hire. His skill and his trusty Sharps rifle had tracked and killed more wolves than any other in the territories bordering the Rockies.

The one-armed man looked to his foreman. "Bill, I want you to ride into Miles City and bring him back here. I want these beasts hunted down and eliminated once and for all. If it takes an expert wolfer to do the job, then I'm willing to hire one. Especially one with the reputation of Timber Gray."

Whittaker noticed Seth standing there, pale with shock. "You might take young Adams with you, if he's feeling up to it. The ride into town might do him some good." The elderly cattleman put his single hand on the cowhand's shoulder. "You doing all right, son?"

Seth nodded. "Yes, sir, Mr. Whittaker. Just a little rattled, that's all. It was just seeing poor Charlie lying there like that…"

"I know, son." Whittaker's lean face was grim. "It's a hard land, Montana is. But to tame it, there have to be sacrifices. Charlie Piper was one of those sacrifices and we'll never forget him for that, now will we?"

"No, sir," answered Seth. "Never will." His reply was echoed by the other men in the room.

As they moved out of the parlor and made their way down the hallway to the main door, Whittaker's resounding voice stopped them. "Bill, do the men go armed while riding the range?"

The bearded foreman nodded. "Just a rifle when they're out line-riding."

"From now on have them wear sidearms as well," he said. Through the open doorway he could see the buckboard waiting with the dead cowhand's shrouded body lying in the back. "I'll not lose another good man to those murderous devils!"

Chapter Three

It happened in the autumn of 1865.

Five months had passed since the surrender at Appomattox courthouse and the South was grudgingly attempting to adjust to the trials of a Northern-imposed reconstruction. Most soldiers had returned home to find their farms burned, their homes destroyed, and their families stricken by disease and poverty.

But it had not been like that for a fortunate few. Those who lived in the wilderness areas of the Appalachian Mountains had found their former lives virtually untouched. Homesteads hidden in the mountain hollows had escaped the scavenging troops of both Union and Confederate forces. The only problem they found—and it soon turned out to be quite a devastating problem—was the sudden lack of food. The roar of wartime cannons and the steady report of musketfire had driven most of the wildlife further westward. Deer, the life's meat of the mountaineer, had fled, leaving only small game and fowl behind as food for both man and more savage predators.

It was a crisp fall day in early October when Jefferson Gray walked a trail through the Smoky Mountains of eastern Tennessee, his spirits high and his day's hunting rewarded. His double-barreled shotgun had dispatched a sizable turkey an hour before and his stride was light as he made his way back home, the gobbler slung over his shoulder.

He came to Chestnut Creek and walked along the clearwater branch. His two-room cabin was only a hoot and a holler away, nestled in a stand of tall, green pines. There his wife would be, baking bread or churning butter, and his young son, Todd, playing around the house. As he continued on his way, Jefferson remembered that today was Rebecca's wash day. She would be somewhere along the creekbed, washing what little linen they owned on the rocks of the babbling brook.

Sounds from up ahead drew his attention. His ears strained against the sound of the trickling stream, trying to sort out the noises. Suddenly they came to him like a slap in the face. There were screams—feminine screams—as well as the frightened cries of a child. And there were other sounds.

Sounds that sent a cold dread coursing through Jefferson Gray's stocky frame. The fierce snaps and snarls of hungry wolves.

He dropped his prized turkey and sprinted along the trail, praying to the good Lord and reloading his twelve-gauge as he ran. He leapt over several deadfalls and tore through a thicket of blackberry bramble before he finally made the creekside clearing. And what he witnessed there beside the peaceful stream of Chestnut Creek made his blood run icy cold.

Three wolves had discovered Gray's family, alone, as they tended to the day's wash. Whether they had been hungry or just looking for something to kill, Gray couldn't say. But they had found them, never the less, and had set upon them with a fevered vengeance that the young mountaineer had never witnessed before. With a hysterical curse on his lips, Jefferson Gray ran out of the canebrake, cocking both hammers of his scattergun.

Rebecca was already dead. They had caught her first, pulling her to the rocky earth and ripping at her with angry fangs until she no longer thrashed and screamed beneath them. Her throat had been torn open and, while two of the wolves went after the boy, a third remained, devouring his share of the easy kill.

Jefferson screamed in horror and raised his shotgun. The first barrel discharged its load, blowing the wolf away from the woman's blood-splattered body. The second shot blew most the animal's head into the forest at the edge of the creek. His muzzleloader empty, he turned away from Rebecca's lifeless form and toward the screams of his son.

He found little Todd further downstream, still on his feet, but the object of two wolves' hellish game of tug-o-war. A wolf had him by each arm, pulling and tearing, trying to drag him off balance. The fair-haired boy's face was streaked with blood and tears. His eyes were glazed with fear, until they spotted his father running down the creekbed, his hands fisted around the gun's double barrels.

"Pa!" screamed the child. "Pa, help me!"

"I'm a-coming, Todd!" the man called. "Just hold on, son!"

As he reached the wolves and their youthful prey, Jefferson swung his shotgun like a club, aiming toward a snarling, gray head. The cherrywood stock met bone with a loud crack and the beast loosened his hold on the child's left arm. The shotgun descended again and again, until the wolf lay dead on the jagged rocks and the stock had splintered in half at the breach.

The other wolf had Todd on the ground now. Jefferson could hear the ripping of his son's clothing and the sickening tear of his flesh. Throwing the useless weapon away. Gray drew a hunting knife from his belt and leapt forward onto the third wolf's back. He plunged the blade into the thick gray fur, withdrew it, plunged again. The wolf rolled over, taking the man with him. Jefferson continued to slash and stab. Blood coated his hands and splattered the front of his buckskin shirt. Finally, he reached around the wolf's thrashing head and cut his throat. The creature thudded into the loose rocks at the edge of Chestnut Creek and died.

"Todd!" rasped Gray, staggering toward his son. But he was too late. The amount of blood and the glassy stare of little Todd's eyes told him that the boy was already beyond hope.

He knelt there, cradling his son in his arms. Angry tears rolled down his whiskered cheeks. "Oh, Todd! Dear God, no! Not both of them!"

So grieved was the man, that he failed to hear the growl of a fourth wolf as it came out of the woods. He didn't even know it was there until the animal knocked him sprawling into the stream. The cold water jolted the mountaineer out of his numbing grief and he found himself once again face to face with a slavering beast. He brought his hand up, but the knife was gone, lost from his fall into the creek. The wolf snapped and snarled, looking more mad than wild with bloodlust. Jefferson felt a searing pain as the canine's fangs bore down on his left forearm, tearing into muscle and bringing a gorge of warm blood.

The sight of his own blood dispelled the man's panic for an instant. He felt around in the water beneath him, perhaps searching for the knife. Instead, his hand closed around a large stone. With the scream of a madman, he lunged with all his might, bringing the rock down forcefully upon the wolf's head. The blow seemed to do no harm to the crazed animal. He pounded again and again. Still the wolf refused to let go.

"You filthy beast!" screamed Jefferson Gray as he reared back and struck again. "Why don't you die? Why don't you die... you... dirty... filthy... beast!"

After a dozen devastating blows, the wolf's hold loosened. After five more, it fell backwards into the branch, its skull no longer resembling the head of a wolf, but an ugly mass of blood and battered brain. With the beast dead, the man dropped his stone back into the churning waters and staggered to his feet.

Jefferson Gray stared down at his arm. The wound was deep, reaching clear down to the bone. But something else disturbed him more than the extent of the fang marks. The blood of the wound was flecked with slaver; a thick coating of saliva that had not washed away in the stream. His dark gray eyes darted to the dead wolf. The animal's snout protruded from the ripples of the creek and, from it, thick foam tinged with blood settled upon the water. In sudden horror, he was hit with the awful reality of what had truly compelled them to act so savagely toward him and his family.

Timber Gray lurched from his fitful sleep, a scream trapped behind clenched teeth. As the remnants of the nightmare began to fade, he breathed deeply and shook off the feeling of near hysteria that had gripped him. He ran his hands over his whiskered face. A cold film of sweat covered his features and he trembled with a palsy of raw nerves.

He turned down the patchwork quilt that covered him and sat on the edge of his bed, feeling his heartbeat slow from its rapid pace. "Damn!" he growled bitterly beneath his breath.

He was no longer in the mountainous Tennessee of 1865, but in a hotel room in Miles City, Montana in the year 1880. Fifteen long years had passed since that horrible incident at Chestnut Creek. Many miles had been traveled since then. Time had passed, but still he had the nightmares. They had come every night the first few years, then became less frequent when he left Tennessee and headed west. But still they resurfaced every now and then, tormenting him, reminding him of Rebecca and Todd… and the wolves.

It was morning. Pale gray light filtered through the single curtained window, casting a murky gloom over the room's interior. Wind whistled around the eaves of the two story hotel. With a groan, he got up, dressed only in faded red longjohns, and padded barefoot across the hardwood floor. He opened the drapes.

Miles City was quiet at six o'clock. The cattle town consisted of a single main street with one and two story false-fronted buildings facing on either side. He saw the faint glow of kerosene lamps in a few windows and there was a sooty billow of woodsmoke coming from the kitchen of O'Brien's Restaurant across the street. Cassie O'Brien would be there now, rolling out some of her famous cathead biscuits for the crowd who would soon appear at her doorstep.

He had almost expected to see snow on the ground. It was surely cold enough and the clouds that rolled over the prairie were dark and oppressive. Not that he cared much either way. He had just come off the trail after spending four months in the Dakotas. His last paying job had been near Fort Buford on the Missouri River. A little place called Hendrich had been having trouble with a feisty mountain lion that had killed several dogs and a small child who had wondered from the safety of town. Gray had brought back the cougar's hide after two day's tracking and was paid half the bounty that was originally promised. For now, he was content to stay put in Miles City for a few weeks, waiting out the storm that was sure to come. There was strong drink, whores, and card games over at the Steerhead

14

Saloon and food a-plenty at O'Brien's to fatten him up before spring thaw.

The prospect of ham and eggs and strong, black coffee brightened his outlook a little and he walked to the bureau across the room. He poured water into the wash basin from a porcelain pitcher and commenced to washing away the clammy sweat of his troubled sleep. Toweling off, he caught his reflection in the oval mirror. He grimaced at the sorry fellow that stared back at him.

Timber Gray was a man of medium height, but stocky in build. His hair was dark, but in more recent years showed an increasing iron grayness around the temples and the scraggly growth of his beard. The skin of his face and hands were deeply lined and dyed a leathery brown from years in the harsh elements of the West. His eyes were dark slate-gray. They were grim eyes, ones that suggested a great deal of hardship and suffering. Eyes that contained the wisdom and frontier savvy of a man much older than his forty-two years.

He dressed, pulled on a pair of scuffed riding boots, and slung a worn gunbelt with a holstered Colt .45 around his waist. Then he donned a heavy sheepskin coat. As he tugged a silverbelly Stetson over his head, a hearty breakfast foremost in his mind, he thought again of the nightmare that had plagued his sleep. From past experience he knew that he only had the dream when something peculiar was about to happen. The dream was an omen of sorts, a premonition of bad times ahead.

With a sigh, Timber Gray started down the stairway to the hotel lobby. He couldn't help but wonder exactly what kind of mess that damned nightmare was going to get him into this time.

Chapter Four

Timber Gray was finishing up his breakfast when two men walked into O'Brien's restaurant. He had noticed them only a few moments before as they rode into town, followed by another cowhand in a wagon. The two had hitched their mounts in front of the Miles City Hotel and gone inside, while the buckboard had continued on up the street to where the town's only church and its graveyard stood on a lonely, treeless hill.

The two were cattlemen. Timber could tell that by the look and smell of them. One was a big man in his early thirties, bearded, wearing a buffalo coat and a gray Montana peak hat. The other was just a boy, no more than eighteen. His youthful face seemed strained and somewhat troubled, as if he'd had a bad scare lately. Both brought the familiar rancher's smell of old leather, cattle, and dried manure through the café door with them.

The big man's brooding eyes studied the room until they finally settled on Gray. As the warmth of the woodstove dispelled the chill of their entrance, he led the way through the maze of crowded eating tables. The young cowboy followed close behind. Timber Gray sopped up the remainder of his meal with a biscuit, looking up only when the two approached his table.

"Pardon me, mister," began the bearded man. "But would you be the wolf hunter… Timber Gray?"

Timber nodded. "I reckon so. And who are you?"

"I'm Bill Brighton, foreman of a ranch southwest of here, and this is Seth Adams. We've come to talk some business with you."

The wolf hunter had ridden into Miles City hoping for a rest from his grueling line of work, but he knew there would be no harm in listening to what these men had to say. "Please, sit down."

As the cattlemen pulled up a couple of chairs and made themselves to home, Timber caught the proprietor's attention. "Mrs. O'Brien, how about bringing these boys a pot of coffee? Looks like they need something strong and hot to take the morning chill outta their bones."

"Right away, Mr. Gray," smiled the Irish woman. She took a stack of empty dishes from a neighboring table and disappeared into the kitchen.

"Well, now, what seems to be your trouble?" he asked, turning his eyes from the young cowpoke to the older veteran.

"Wolves, Mr. Gray," replied Bill Brighton. "Timber wolves."

"My specialty." The hunter was well known for his proficiency at tracking the wood-born animals, and therefore had rightly earned his nickname from it. "They've been after your cattle?"

Bill nodded grimly. "Taken sixteen head in the last month. But that ain't the worst of it. Last night they set upon one of our men. He and his horse were both torn to shreds. Killed."

17

Timber was not surprised by the wolves' killing of a human being. Though the incidents were few and far between, wolves had been known to turn from their normal prey of deer, to attack cattle and, sometimes, man. Usually it had to do with hunger, anger, or cornered desperation. Many times the killings had no justification whatsoever. Sometimes the animal just felt the bloodthirsty urge to kill. Timber knew that fact better than most men, for he had seen the ugly sight of needless death in the past, both in Tennessee and the hostile country west of the Mississippi River.

Cassie O'Brien appeared at their table, setting a coffee pot and two porcelain cups before them. She frowned in disapproval at the two cowhands. "I'd surely appreciate it if ye'd remove yer hats, gentlemen. This is a respectable eating establishment, not some cattle drive chuckwagon."

"Pardon us, ma'am." Bill nudged Seth and they both hurriedly removed their headgear. Soon the coffee was poured and the hot brew worked to settle their nerves and warm their chilled bodies.

Timber sipped a couple of swallows of tar black coffee from his refilled cup and returned to the matter at hand. "Exactly how large is this pack? How many wolves are we talking about?"

The foreman hesitated. He traded a worried glance with Seth, then answered. "Well, from the tracks and the few times we've actually seen the critters, I'd have to be fair in saying there's close to fifty."

The number surprised the wolfer. Sure, he had tracked dozens of packs before, but none of them had numbered more than fifteen or twenty. A pack of fifty was indeed a number to be reckoned with. To most men, a lone hunter going after such a pack would be suicidal. Better for a posse of an armed dozen to go after them. But Timber Gray did not think much of hunting parties. He worked as a loner and, despite the odds, always tracked and found the prey he had set out for. But, *fifty* timber wolves! The sheer weight of that number both frightened and intrigued the seasoned hunter.

And there was something else, something in the back of his mind that troubled Timber. He thought of the nightmare and of the trouble it always seemed to bring in its wake. That, the number of the marauding pack, and the approaching blizzard made him increasingly apprehensive about accepting the job.

"You're awful quiet, son," he said, looking at Seth. The boy met his questioning gaze and the wolfer saw that there was fire hidden in those saddened eyes.

"Yes, sir, I surely am," said the cowboy. "You see, I found a man murdered this morning… a man I bunked and ate with for nearly two years. I found him in a lonesome cow pasture with his gullet torn open and his innards drug plumb outta his belly. It sickened me, mister, and most of all, it angered me. That's why I rode into town with Bill. We were hoping you'd help us get those damned wolves, on account Mr. Whittaker can't spare us to do the job."

Suddenly, Timber Gray's eyes brightened with fresh interest. "Whittaker? You fellas wouldn't happen to work for Louis B. Whittaker, would you?"

"Yes, we do," said Brighton. "He sent us into town to get you. Said he'd talk money as soon as you got out to the ranch."

The hunter settled back in his chair and ran a hand thoughtfully over the coarse bristles of his gray-streaked beard. "Lou Whittaker… that old son of a pistol!" he said, his eyes full of remembrance. He grinned and found himself chuckling in spite of himself.

"Know Mr. Whittaker, do you?"

Timber nodded. "From way back." At the two men's curious stares, he elaborated. "Let's just say that we fought for the same cause at one time."

The Whittaker hands nodded. They both knew of their boss's involvement in the War Between the States. "Does that mean you'll take the job?" asked Seth hopefully.

"It means I'm willing to listen to what the Colonel has to say," replied Timber Gray. He pushed himself up from the table, shrugged on his sheepskin coat, and tugged the silverbelly hat over his head. "And if I remember Lou Whittaker right, he'll more than likely be able to talk me into it."

Chapter Five

L ouis Whittaker watched from the window as three riders rode onto the ranch from the direction of town. Two of them were Brighton and Adams, while the third was a stranger on a black gelding with three white stockings. It was nearing noon, but the sun had not yet made its appearance and wouldn't until the boiling clouds overhead dumped their frozen load across the grassy Montana plains.

The cattleman watched as the three tied their mounts to the hitching post outside the bunkhouse and then started across the frozen yard toward the two-story plantation-style house. Whittaker recognized the man immediately. True, it had been nearly seventeen years, but the one he had known as Captain Jefferson Gray confirmed the old memories never the less. He remembered him being a little too rawboned and reckless for one befitting a proper officer of the Confederacy, but, otherwise, he was one hell of a fighting man. It had been Jefferson Gray who had continued the cavalry charge when Whittaker had fallen at Murfreesboro.

The cattle baron turned from the window and crossed the room to a bookcase packed with classic novels and manuals on stock breeding. The center shelf held a locked, glass door. Whittaker took a key from his vest pocket and unlocked the cabinet, revealing a small bar stocked with the finest liquors. He adjusted his string tie and the black jacket over the stump of his lost arm as the sound of men entering the house reached the front parlor.

Brighton appeared at the door first, then Adams and the wolf hunter. "We're back, Mr. Whittaker, and we brought along the wolfer, Timber Gray."

"Thank you, Bill," said Whittaker. "Could you two please leave me and Mr. Gray alone for a while? We have some pressing business to discuss."

The foreman nodded and closed the door behind him as they left. The two men stood there in the parlor and looked each other over for a long moment. Then, Timber walked across the room, his hat off and his hand extended.

"It's good to see you again, Colonel," he said with a grin, shaking the only good hand the elderly man possessed. "Why, the last time I laid eyes on you, you'd been hit by a cannonball at Stones River. Me and the boys fought those Yanks, but by the time we got back, the medics had taken you off. We didn't hear a thing concerning you after that. I reckon we figured you for dead… until now."

"It takes more than Union shot to drop a tough, old bird like me, Captain."

He laughed and flapped the armless sleeve of his coat. "Just winged me, that's all." Whittaker walked over to the bar and brought out a crystal decanter and two shotglasses. "How about a drink? I received a bottle of French cognac as a Christmas gift. I was saving it for a special occasion, but I suppose this reunion qualifies as such."

"Should be quite a treat for an old whiskey-guzzler like myself," said Timber.

The cattleman poured the brandy, then the two men raised their glasses. "A toast," offered Whittaker. "To our glorious and rightful Cause. Let us never forget the brave men who fought and died for it."

"Amen to that," agreed Timber. The cognac tasted strange and didn't pack the wallop that good ol' Redeye did. He reckoned he'd rather have had a stiff shot of Tennessee sourmash in his glass than that fancy foreign stuff any old day.

The hunter sat on a red velvet sofa, while Whittaker took a leather armchair. All remembrances of the past were put aside. The grisly matter at hand filled the room with an awkward silence.

"I hear you have wolf trouble, Colonel."

"That's putting it mildly," said Whittaker. "There is a pack of nearly fifty timber wolves traveling across my land. They kill in excess, eat their fill, then move onward. They keep to the woods and appear only when easy prey presents itself. What I need from you, Jefferson, is your help and your expertise. I want you to hunt the pack down and kill every last one of those murdering scoundrels."

Timber Gray took out the makings and began to roll himself a cigarette. "Your foreman, Brighton, told me that the wolves have hamstrung close to sixteen head."

"That's true. But that's not the reason I'm hiring you to go after them. Sixteen head isn't even considered a loss in my tally book. I'll have close to ten thousand head by spring roundup. What really sticks in my craw is that they killed one of my finest hands. Charlie Piper was a good man and I'll be damned if I'll let those bloodthirsty beasts escape, just to kill someone else."

Timber nodded in complete understanding. As he had ridden to the Whittaker ranch with the two cowhands, the wolfer had wondered if the Colonel wanted the wolves tracked for the purely economical reason of saving a few cows. Most cattlemen did. But it turned out that Whittaker's motive was more honorable than selfish. Like most men who dealt with the cattle business, Timber Gray also despised the wolves that preyed upon the helpless to feed the strong, even though it was the way of nature. The wolfer was much more involved when human victims were at stake. It was the burning memory of what had happened beside that mountain stream in 1865 that drove Gray to kill every wolf he came in contact with, whether hired to do so or not.

"You know there's a mighty bad storm heading in from the north," pointed out Timber. "If I was to start out after those wolves today, that blizzard would catch up with me before I could even get a third of the job done."

Whittaker took a money roll big enough to choke a Missouri mule from out of his coat pocket. "I know that. That's why I'll offer you an even thousand dollars in cash money right here and now. Also, I'll throw in a couple of good horses and any supplies you might need. Does that sound fair enough?"

"Sure it does, Colonel. Normally I'd jump at such an offer. But, still, I'm gonna have to say no." Timber's thoughts were lingering on dangers other than that snowstorm. Again, he recalled the nightmare, remembered the way it served as an omen for hard times ahead. The last time he had the dream, a grizzly bear had nearly mauled him to death in the Rockies. This time his shortsightedness could mean being torn to shreds by timber wolves in the frozen wilds of southwestern Montana.

Whittaker could see the reluctance in the hunter's eyes. He poured himself another shot of the fancy French liquor and took a long, thoughtful sip. "All right, I'm willing to sweeten the pot a bit. In addition to the thousand dollars, I'll pay you twenty dollars for each wolf hide you bring back to me. No cattleman west of Kansas City is going to offer you a deal like that."

The wolfer knew that he was right. The going bounty on wolf hides at that time was five dollars apiece. Whittaker was offering a tempting profit of fifteen dollars per hide. And with a pack numbering close to fifty, that was pretty hard to pass up, storm or no storm.

"That would come to quite a piece of money, Colonel."

"Yes, it would. Enough to last you through quite a few winters." Whittaker leaned forward in his chair, anxious to learn his friend's decision. "So, what will it be, Jefferson? Will you do this job for me?"

Timber stood and pulled on his hat. "Do those supplies include a new set of guns and ammunition? My old Colt and Winchester are mighty worn after all the use I've put them through in the last few years."

"Of course," assured the one-armed man. "And I'll even throw in some cartridges for that Sharps buffalo gun you've got hanging on your saddle."

"Then I reckon you've got yourself a deal," said Timber Gray.

He and Whittaker shook hands to consummate the deal and the cattle baron accompanied him down the hall to the front door. "Bill and Seth, they'll let you pick the horses and whatever gear you need. Then I'll have one of them ride out with you to my Spruce Valley line station. That's the direction those wolves were heading this morning. I've got several thousand head down in the valley there and I'd bet my best pair of Sunday boots that is where they'll attack next."

After another warm handshake, Timber Gray left the company of the old man. He crossed the rutted ranchyard to the bunkhouse. He lingered beside his horse for a moment before going inside to the toasty warmth of a potbelly stove. He breathed in the aroma of cold horse and aged leather as he stood beside the animal, letting his gloved hand rest absently on the jutting stock of the old Sharps. Abruptly, a cold northern wind blew across the plains. It engulfed him, rustling his clothing and numbing the exposed skin of his face.

Casting the butt of his cigarette aside, he turned and walked up the steps to the bunkhouse door. Behind him, the wind seemed to howl a mournful warning, as if cautioning him of dangers that lay ahead.

It was a sound he had heard often, but one he rarely listened to. A warning that eluded the stubborn wolfer until it was entirely too late to take heed.

Chapter Six

The ride to Spruce Valley took the remainder of the day. After leaving the main acreage of the Whittaker ranch with its sparse buildings and cattle-filled corrals, the land gave way to the abandonment of the still Montana plains. The grasslands were plentiful near the muddy vein of the Powder River, then turned into more rugged terrain as they stretched further southwest toward the valley cache of cattle that the wolf pack was most likely to strike next.

Timber Gray urged his black gelding across the barren Montana earth. His guide, Seth Adams, rode close beside him. Gray had felt a little uneasy upon leaving Miles City, but now, riding the open plains with the bite of the January wind on his face, he once again felt in control. This was his place in life, be it Montana flatland or Colorado highland. In the wilderness there were only the elements of nature to contend with. No slick-handed poker players, no gun-happy drunkards… just he and his prey. Timber was a man leery of crowds and, although Miles City wasn't as big a town as many, he knew he would have probably packed his saddlebags and left in a day or so anyway, snow or no snow.

The wolfer was in high spirits that day, most of that wellbeing due to the generosity of Louis Whittaker. Timber had a thousand dollars in his possession, with the promise of that much more at the end of the hunt. Behind him followed two sturdy pack horses loaded with a month's worth of supplies. His old short-barreled Colt had been replaced with a spanking new .45 and the boot on the right side of his saddle sported a fresh Winchester .44-40. His saddlebags were stocked with spare ammunition, including cartridges for his .50 Sharps long gun.

From early afternoon until the gradual darkening of evening, the ride had been laden with silence. But as the miles lessened between them and their destination, so did the extent of their private thoughts. Seth began to tell the elder man of his family back on the Texas Panhandle. He told Gray of his pa's ranch near Amarillo, of his ma and three sisters. And there were two older brothers; one of them a marshal in the Arizona territory, the other a no-account horse thief who had been rightfully hung in Kansas back in 1877.

Timber Gray didn't mind the boy's rambling talk. In his travels, the wolfer had met many people, but had made few friends. Here, on the lonely ride to Spruce Valley, he had begun to take a liking to this Texas-born cowhand named Seth Adams. But the friendship seemed to be linked to a darker side of the wolf hunter. Seth reminded him of the man little Todd might have become if he had survived that horrible day in the wilds of the Smoky Mountains.

The clouds that boiled overhead grew darker and denser, bringing twilight earlier than usual. They crested a rise and saw the vast expanse of the valley below them. Whittaker's estimate of the cattle had been correct. It looked as though several thousand head grazed on the rolling pastures of brown grass. The Tongue River ran along the western side of the valley, while to the southwest stood a thick forest of pine and blue spruce. On the edge of that forest was a small cabin; the line station Whittaker had told Gray about earlier.

Their destination finally in sight, they made their way through the herd toward the inviting glow of a kerosene lamp and the acrid aroma of woodsmoke. The one-roomed cabin was constructed of roughly hewn logs chinked with mud and sod. To the side was an overhang where tools and harnesses hung, as well as a few hay-littered stalls for the horses.

The two riders reached the shelter and tied their horses in a couple of stalls, removing their weapons and saddlebags. They were in the process of unsaddling their mounts, when the door opened and two men stepped gingerly into the chill of the winter twilight.

"How you been doing, Seth?" greeted a lanky man with a handlebar mustache. He shook the boy's hand, then eyed Timber Gray with good-natured interest.

"Well enough, Tom," replied Seth. "That is, up until today, I reckon."

"Yah, we heard of poor Charlie," said the other man, his voice heavy with the accent of a foreign land. He was a huge man and his hair and beard was long and golden blond, reminding Timber of the Vikings of ancient Norway that his father had told him stories about during his childhood.

Tom nodded grimly. "Ralph Walker rode out and told us about it. Terrible thing what happened to Charlie. But, dammit, I knew it was bound to happen sooner or later. Confounded wolves!"

"That's why we're here. This is the man the boss hired to hunt down that murdering pack. And believe you me, he hired the best."

Tom studied the wolfer carefully in the light of the open doorway. His grin broadened slightly. "You're Timber Gray, ain't you?"

The hunter hoisted his gelding's saddle off its back and set it on the railing of the stall fence. "That's right."

"Pleasure to meet you." The lanky cowhand stepped forward and shook Gray's hand. It seemed as though the wolfer had traded more handshakes that day than he had in the last few years. "I'm Tom McCorkendale and this hefty fella here is Big Swede."

After unburdening the two pack horses, the four retired to the warmth of the line station. The cabin's interior was lit by a single coal oil lamp and the flickering glow of a stone hearth. The walls were covered with yellowed newspaper and pages from old mail-order catalogs, insulating the cabin's occupants from the chilly drafts of late January. *Why,* thought Timber, *a man could read to his heart's content all winter long and never come across the same wall twice.*

"Hope you boys are hungry," said Tom. "Swede's cooking up a mess of venison and beans, and we've got plenty of hot coffee to wash it down with."

"Yeah, I've heard tell of the Swede's coffee," said Seth with a mischievous twinkle in his eye. "They say you can float a blacksmith's anvil in that stuff."

Big Swede waved his camp knife at the boy, a look of disapproval on his massive face. "Watch your tongue, youngster, or it could very well end up cooking in this pot of beans."

"I almost believe he means it, Seth," laughed McCorkendale. "Lately, old Swede's been pretty cantankerous. I do believe he's got a touch of the cabin fever."

"Bah!" growled the big man, turning back to the preparation of the meal.

30

Timber Gray dumped his gear in a far corner, then shed his coat and hat. "I reckon you fellas haven't seen any sign of that wolf pack, have you?"

"Not yet," replied Big Swede as he stooped over his kettle. "But they are near."

"How do you know that?"

The bearded man shrugged. "It is a feeling I have. When I was a child in my native Sweden, I felt the nearness of wolves. I knew when they prowled the forest outside our village and I was always right. Do not ask me to explain it, for I cannot."

"In that case, I think we ought to ride herd," suggested Tom. "At least until they decide to make their move."

"Good idea." Timber accepted a mug of steaming coffee from the big cook. "I'll be glad to ride a shift, if necessary."

"No need for that. Rest up. You're gonna need all your strength when you go after them. Me and Seth, we'll ride tonight. I'll take the first shift, Seth the second. Four hours each."

"Sounds fine to me," said the young cowhand. He sat on a bunk, his rifle resting across his knees.

"Eat it while it's hot," said Big Swede as he set a simmering cauldron of beans in the center of a sturdy plank table. They all pulled up the benches and hungrily sat down to the modest feast at hand.

Chapter Seven

There was no moon to speak of that night. If there was one, it was well hidden by the black fleece of stormclouds that moved in, slowly but surely, from the north. The pastureland of Spruce Valley was dark, the surrounding stands of timber even darker. The only sounds to be heard were the sounds natural to any Montana cow camp; the soft milling of cattle, the rush of the nearby Tongue River, and the mournfully cold howl of the winter wind.

Tom McCorkendale's watch had ended two hours ago. It was now Seth Adams' turn to keep vigil. The young cowhand rode a steady circle around the big herd, engulfed in a thick blanket of dense darkness. One of his gloved hands was fisted around the Winchester that laid ready across his lap, while the other held steady to the reigns of the bay.

Seth Adams had ridden herd many a time in the dead of winter. Comfort was rare on the cattle plains, whether it be in Montana or the Panhandle. It was no different on the vast expanse of the Whittaker spread. Seth had been born of a hard Texas family, accustomed to trouble and responsibility. He had never minded riding winter herd... until tonight. He couldn't account for his sudden uneasiness and that bothered him. Perhaps it was the inky darkness and the chill wind that heightened his senses, tightening his nerves to their straining point. That and the danger of the wolves that very well might be lurking, hidden from view, in the black timber of the surrounding forest.

He urged his horse onward, heading along the western side of the valley. When he had relieved McCorkendale earlier, the veteran hand had told him that everything looked calm enough. The cattle seemed easy and unconcerned, where they would have been skittish if the wild scent of wolf had been pungent enough to reach them on the gusts of the winter wind.

The cowboy was beginning to think that the wolves had passed them by, when he sensed that something was wrong. Up ahead the cattle were becoming restless. The slow milling had turned into a steady surge toward the center of the valley, as if the cows closest to the wooded boundary were attempting to keep their distance from some menace.

The cattle's exodus made Seth urge his horse into a trot. His heart began to beat faster as his own mount began to shy away with nervous excitement. He squinted into the darkness beyond the few remaining cows at that end of the pasture, desperately trying to search out the cause of the animals' sudden agitation.

Then, through the sweeping rush of the night wind, he heard the howling of wolves. The mournful sound had always sent shivers down Seth's spine, but the wailing he heard now increased that feeling a hundred-fold. It began with the call of one wolf, was joined by four more, then a dozen. Suddenly, the howling filled the basin of Spruce Valley, seeming to encompass it on all sides. Seth's horse bucked and turned, its eyes wild with panic.

"Easy, boy," whispered Seth, leaning forward in his saddle and running a comforting hand along the side of the bay's broad neck. "We'll get outta this in one piece. Don't you worry none."

But the horse was more concerned with the wolf scent in its nostrils than the soft words of its rider. It twisted suddenly toward the direction of the fleeing cows. At that moment, Seth caught a glimpse of a lone steer running toward the river, bellowing loudly in fear. Two pale forms, long and low to the ground, flashed through the darkness in hot pursuit. Two hungry wolves swiftly gaining on their prey.

Seth brought the Winchester to his shoulder, levering a cartridge into the breach and sighting carefully down the barrel. When he had drawn a bead on the wolf nearest the cow, he squeezed off a shot. The bullet found its mark. The timber wolf tumbled, snoot over tail, a .44 slug buried deep in the back of its skull. The other wolf leapt over its fallen sibling and continued on. Seth was about to fire again, when his bay began to buck beneath him in throes of panic, fear, and pain.

There was a wolf at the horse's hindquarters, its fangs flashing, tearing at the flesh of the bay's ankles. Seth twisted awkwardly, trying to take aim on the wolf. But before he could fire, the gelding reared and he went spinning from the saddle. The cowhand hit the frozen ground hard. With a groan, he picked himself up, shaking off dizziness and trying to regain his lost breath. He saw his horse galloping off into the night with the wolf still ripping savagely at his legs. Seth could have gotten a quick shot off, but he found his hands empty. He had lost the Winchester during his fall and had no idea where it was.

"Dammit!" declared the boy. "I ain't gonna end up like Charlie did!" He slipped the thong off the hammer of his Colt and drew the revolver from its holster.

All of the cattle had shifted toward the middle of the valley and Seth found himself alone on the grassy plain. Darkness surrounded him on all sides, combined with the unnerving sounds of bawling cows and the rushing waters of the Tongue. The howling had let off until only a few wolves continued the cry.

Abruptly, guttural growls erupted to Seth's right and he swung his .45 in that direction. The pale gray flash of a thickly-furred form lurched out of the blackness. For a split second, Seth could see the wolf's face, furious and hungry, its eyes sparkling like silver coins, its teeth bared. The beast leapt just as the cowpoke thumbed back the hammer and leveled the Colt's barrel. The report of the gun was deafening. The wolf kept coming and, at first, Seth was certain that he had missed his mark. He yelled out in alarm and stumbled backwards. The canine hit the earth rolling, however, and stopped in a quivering heap, most of its face blown away.

Seth pulled his eyes from the dead wolf and directed them toward the night once again. Two more wolves came toward him cautiously, but still driven by the same bloodlust possessed by their fallen brother.

"Come on!" he yelled in defiance. "Come on, you filthy critters! I'm ready for you!" His hand trembled as he steadied his pistol.

The wolves rushed forward, advancing as one. Seth was about to fire, but he never pulled the trigger. There was a deep-throated growl close behind him and, before he could even turn, he felt the heat of a wolf's breath prickling the hairs on the back of his neck.

Chapter Eight

Timber Gray's eyes snapped open at the first sounds of the howling.

"They're here," he said, loud enough to rouse the others. Then he hurriedly pulled on his trousers and boots.

The cabin was dark except for the last glowing embers of the hearth. The hunter could hear soft swearing and the rustling of clothing as McCorkendale and Big Swede dressed and found their guns. He bucked his own gunbelt around his waist and took his rifle out of the corner by his bunk.

"We'd best get out there and lend Seth a hand," said Tom. The cowpoke slipped a long coat over his lean frame and tugged on his hat.

"Yah," agreed the swede. The big man checked a Remington .44 and stuck it in his belt. "I think he is going to need it."

The three of them were leaving the cabin when they heard the echoing crack of Seth's Winchester break through the howl of the winter wind. They wasted no time with saddles. They led their horses from the lean-to stable and mounted them bareback. They had ridden only a few hundred yards into the valley when they heard a second shot, this one from a six-shooter.

"Over yonder!" motioned Tom, his voice booming against the growing commotion. "He's over yonder near the river!"

The three riders spurred their horses into a gallop toward the western end of Spruce Valley. They were halfway there when the cattle lunged out of the darkness, their nostrils flared and their eyes wide with panic. Having no reigns to hold the horses steady, the men grabbed fistfuls of mane and hung on for dear life. The herd came on, splitting in the wake of the three riders, but keeping them from going anywhere.

"Damn these cows!" swore Tom. "We gotta get to Seth... fast!"

Even in the darkness, Timber could see the frightened determination in the cowhand's eyes. The same look was evident in the Big Swede's bearded features. The wolfer knew they were all thinking the same thing. They had the unfortunate Charlie Piper on their minds and knew very well that Seth Adams could end up that way, too.

"The herd is thinning!" said Big Swede.

He was right. The cattle were spreading now and the center, where the riders were caught, was sparse enough to ride through. They urged their mounts forward, dodging stray cows and searching the dark flatland ahead for some sign of the boy.

Seth's scream hit them all like a blow to the gut. Hearts pounded and hands filled with blued steel as they ran their horses to the limit. The young cowhand's agonized wails lasted only an instant. Then there were only the distant snarls of wolves somewhere on the far side of the valley.

"Confound it!" said Tom. Anger twisted his face into an ugly scowl. "We're too late! They've already gotten to him!"

They reached a small dip in the pasture and, upon topping a steady rise, came upon the wolves. There must have been a dozen of them on the sprawled body of Seth Adams, and a dozen more on the bucking form of the bay gelding. Other wolves swarmed across the frozen grass, chasing cattle and feeding upon those unlucky enough to have fallen.

"Good God Almighty!" gasped Tom McCorkendale. "Will you look at them?" It was clear to see that he had never encountered so many wolves in one place in all his born days.

Timber Gray was also shocked at the sheer number of the pack, but did not let it numb him into immobility. He slid off the back of his horse, knelt, and took aim with the fluid motion of a seasoned hunter. He shot one wolf through the heart, levered another round into the Winchester, and put another slug through a second wolf's right eye.

The reports of deadly firepower finally had the desired effect. The pack began to disperse and vanish into the night like streaks of silver lightning across the dark earth. Tom and Big Swede were off their mounts now and firing after the fleeing wolves. Swede's pistol found no targets, while Tom's scattergun only grazed a wolf, sending it wounded and peppered with buckshot into the blackness.

The men ran toward Seth's still body, sidestepping several gutted cows, and stopped a few feet from the murdered hand. They stared at his torn body, glistening with blood and exposed bone, then turned away in anger and horror. That was, except for Timber Gray. He let his rifle muzzle droop to the ground and knelt silently beside the young cowhand he had taken a liking to in such a short time.

The wolfer laid his rifle gently on the earth beside him. Reaching across the blood-soaked body, he took a fistful of gray fur and drug a slain wolf off the towheaded boy from Texas. With a grunt of rage, Timber heaved the beast away and regarded the cowhand sadly. The boy's body had been eaten at, but his youthful face had been untouched. It was Seth's glazed eyes—the eyes of a frightened child—that reached deep down into Timber Gray's soul and tore open an old wound. Once again he saw the resemblance of his lost son in the Texan's freckled face.

"Todd," whispered Gray, emotion rising hot in the back of his throat. "Oh, Todd, not again!"

Tom McCorkendale stepped forward and stared at the wolfer in puzzlement. "What did you say, Timber?"

The agonized memory lingered with Timber for a moment more, then faded. But the anger stayed, along with the old hatred. He stood up and canted the rifle over his broad shoulder. "It's just such a waste. Such a damned awful waste."

Tom nodded bitterly. They watched as Big Swede brought Seth's horse back by the reigns. The bay was wild with pain, and no wonder. The horse's back legs, from hooves to hindquarters, had been stripped of flesh by the teeth of the blood-hungry wolves.

"This animal, it is badly hurt," said the Swede. The big man's apparent love of horses could be seen in the pained expression in his crystal blue eyes. "I am afraid he must be…"

"Yeah, I know," said Tom. "Stand back." As soon as Big Swede had released the bay, McCorkendale shouldered his twelve-gauge and fired the remaining barrel. The charge took off the top of the injured horse's head. The animal's body struck the frozen ground with a heavy thud.

"What a hellish night this has turned out to be!" said Big Swede. His beefy face was as pale and haggard as those of the other men.

Timber Gray breathed in deeply, attempting to ignore the stench of fresh blood, and stared to the southwest. That was the direction the wolves had fled to. A lush forest of spruce and pine grew ten miles along the Tongue River; a timbered haven for the escaping pack. But it would not hide them for very long. There were forty-six wolves left now and such a number would leave tracks easy to follow. Gray hoped to catch up to the pack and dispatch at least a few of them before the blizzard hit, if he left right away.

"It'll be light in a couple of hours," he told the two. "I'm gonna prepare my horses and be ready to follow their trail by daybreak." He started across the pasture, toward the line station.

"What about these wolves?" asked Tom.

"Skin the four, take the hides to Whittaker, and collect the eighty dollars bounty," Timber told him. "Give poor Seth a fitting burial, then send the rest of the money to his folks in Amarillo, along with my regrets."

McCorkendale nodded grimly. "We'll surely do that, Timber. But just promise me one thing, will you?"

"What's that?"

"Kill as many of those stinking wolves as you can! Don't let them do in Wyoming what they've gotten away with here in Montana."

"That was what I was hired to do," said Timber Gray. But he knew it went deeper than that now. Much deeper.

Chapter Nine

Timber Gray stood on a stony ridge near the Montana-Wyoming border.

He took a pair of old field glasses from his saddlebags and, lifting them to his eyes, focused on the floor of a narrow ravine that stretched between twin lines of timber. There, near a stream, the pack had hamstrung a large elk. A few wolves still lingered around the empty carcass, devouring the few scraps of meat that remained. The others laid about in leisure, while a group of young males chased one another playfully.

The hunter counted them with the help of the binoculars. Yes, they were all there, all forty-six of them.

A day and a half had passed since Timber left the line station at Spruce Valley. He had followed their trail along the curving channel of the Tongue River, then due south as the pack took to a dense forest that stretched toward the Wyoming territory. The wolves had split up several times, then regrouped; something that Gray had never known a pack to do before. That action alone made it obvious that the pack knew it was being hunted and that its leader was much more cunning and dangerous than the majority of wolves Timber had tracked during the past fifteen years.

He centered his attention on a large group of about eighteen that stood beneath the gnarled limbs of an old sycamore tree. There was one wolf among them, older but larger than the others, that Timber figured to be the leader. The wolf's coat was white with age, but other than that the hunter could not make out any other distinguishing features. After all, Timber was a good distance away, hidden where the pack could not catch his scent or glimpse him on the rocky rise above.

Careful to make no noise, Timber Gray climbed off the ledge to where his horses stood grazing in a hollow only a hundred yards away. Now was the time to act, while the wolves' bellies were full and their movements sluggish. He took a moment to chew a bite of jerky and gulp down a swallow from his canteen. Then he went to work… patiently and without any indication of being in a hurry.

He took a cartridge belt from one of the horses' packs and slung it over his left shoulder. The long brass casings of the .50-140 cartridges were slotted in the belt's loops. He then pulled the Winchester rifle from its boot, levered a round into the breach, and tucked it under his arm. The last thing he took before heading back up the scrubby deer path to the ridge was the Sharps buffalo gun. The breach-loading rifle was built for taking down game at long ranges. Although it was originally intended for such large game as buffalo or moose, Timber had found it just as effective when bringing down wolves.

Reaching his spot on the ridge, he took another quick glance through the field glasses. Only a couple of wolves had shifted their positions. It was clear that they intended to stay there a while and rest off their meal before moving onward.

Timber laid his rifles on a broad, flat stone; the Winchester first, then the .50 long gun. He slid six cartridges from the belt and stood them, one by one, in a line near the Sharps. The lever action was already loaded, holding seventeen rounds in its tubular magazine.

He took another long look through the glasses, then stuck them back in the saddlebags. He had already determined his first target. It was a lone wolf closest to the ridge, a wolf that had been abandoned because of the crippling wound in its left rear haunches. Tom McCorkendale's buckshot had found its mark that night at Spruce Valley, but the shotgun pellets had only grazed the fleeing wolf. That was the main reason Timber decided to take him out first. Even though the wolfer held a strong dislike for the creatures, he did not enjoy seeing any animal suffer from a hunter's misplaced shot.

Timber Gray took his time preparing for the first shot, for he knew when that first wolf dropped, the rest would be hellbent for the cover of the surrounding forest. He cast a slow study around the sprawling countryside. It was quiet, almost serene, the air crisp and cold. The stormy winds of a few nights ago had died down to a gentle breeze, but the heavy mat of dark clouds was growing more threatening overhead. More than likely, the Whittaker ranch was already under a few feet of snow. Timber knew it wouldn't be long before he saw some of it himself.

After pulling a pair of worn deerskin gloves over his hands, he reached over for the Winchester. The hunter lay prone near the lip of the rock shelf.

Resting the rifle's barrel atop his doubled saddlebags, he set the curved buttplate solidly against his shoulder. The bristles of his graying beard rasped on the wood of the stock as he pressed his face to the cheekpiece.

The wounded wolf stood no more than a hundred yards away. Timber centered the front and rear sights on his first target. He breathed in deeply and relaxed. The wolf limped a few feet, then twisted its head around to lick at the buckshot wound. That was when the hunter steadied his aim and squeezed back on the trigger.

The shot cracked through the stillness of the ravine. It echoed across the grassy clearing and into the dense growth of long-leafed pine. The pack forgot their leisure, jerking their heads toward the direction of the rocky rise. They watched as their injured brother slumped to his side, the top of his head blown away by the .44 bullet.

Timber already had his rifle levered for another shot when the pack rose to their feet as one. They began to head for the safety of the forest, just as the wolfer had predicted. He shifted his sights a fraction of an inch and fired again. A she-wolf was caught in the back by the second shot. The slug snapped her spine cleanly and she rolled several times before lying dead in the brown grass.

A third shot followed. It found a wolf as it crossed the clearwater stream. The beast was in mid-bound when the slug burrowed through the heavy fur, lodging deep into the muscle of its heart. The wolf hit the churning water with a magnificent splash and lay there, ice cold water washing its life's blood downstream. Timber Gray fired a fourth time, but the shot fell short, kicking up earth a yard behind the wolf it had been intended for.

The pack had escaped the Winchester's range. Now it was the Sharps' turn. Timber stood from his prone position and picked up the single shot rifle. Skillfully, he unlatched the triggerguard and dropped the breach open. A .50 cartridge was placed in the chamber, then the breach was closed. The hunter crouched to one knee on the stony ledge and brought the heavy gun to his shoulder. He flipped a rear tang sight up into position, adjusting it for greater accuracy. When the heavy octagon barrel was steadied and the target determined, the wolfer cocked the hammer, then pulled back smoothly on the trigger.

The Sharps sounded like a cannon compared to the Winchester. A wolf fell a good three hundred yards away, dispatched by the Sharps' big 700 grain bullet. Timber peered intently through the pall of sulfurous gunsmoke, reloading as he chose his next mark.

Three more wolves fell to the Sharps before the remainder of the pack disappeared into the woods. The wolf hunter had hoped to take out the lead wolf—the old one with the white coat—but it had been one of the first to reach cover. A breeze dispersed the cloud of gunsmoke that hung around Gray. He stood staring down at the results of his handywork. Six wolves lay on the grassy floor of the ravine, and one in the stream. He looked toward the thick forest, satisfied. The pack now numbered thirty-nine. Still a formidable number, but at least down by eleven.

The wolfer reached inside his sheepskin coat, unbuttoned the pocket of his flannel shirt, and took out the makings. He slowly rolled himself a cigarette. After lighting it, he stooped and gathered his rifles and saddlebags. The two unfired cartridges were returned to the belt where they would wait until Old Reliable was again called upon to do its owner's bidding.

Timber Gray climbed off the ridge and made his way down the hollow to where his horses were picketed. He slid the rifles back into their scabbards, then led the gelding and the two pack horses over a narrow deer trail. They reached the ravine a short while later. The horses were skittish at first, the smell of wolves and fresh blood strong in their nostrils. But soon they realized there was no danger present... only death.

The wolfer went to one horse and began to rearrange the supplies in the canvas-shrouded pack, making room for the skins that would soon be lashed there. Tossing his half-smoked cigarette aside, Gray drew a bone-handled skinning knife from a sheath at his belt and went to work on the first wolf.

––––––––––––

Timber awoke the next morning to find snow on the ground.

The dreaded storm that he had eluded since leaving the boundaries of the Whittaker spread had finally caught up to him. He sat up in the lean-to he had constructed from fallen limbs and pine boughs the night before and looked out across a clearing near a stand of scraggly fir trees. A heavy blanket of virgin snow covered the ground and the limbs of trees hung low with its weight. It wasn't snowing the hour of Gray's awakening, but the sudden drop in temperature and the sharpness of the wind told him that last night's snowfall was nothing compared to what would soon follow.

Timber Gray yawned and turned his blankets aside. He still wore his sheepskin coat and gunbelt over his traveling clothes. He stood up and, slipping on his hat, stepped outside the makeshift shelter.

The three horses stood picketed beneath a thick growth of white pine. He was glad that he had anticipated the chance of bad weather, putting them in the shelter of the grove instead of out in the open. Breathing in the frigid air, Timber went to one of the packs and took out a pound of coffee and the tin pot to boil it in.

He started back for the shelter, but stopped for a moment, his gray eyes lingering thoughtfully over the countryside of northern Wyoming. Ahead of him lay miles of thick timberland; the perfect place for a pack of wolves to vanish into thin air. The snow that covered the ground had also erased any tracks that Gray could have followed, therefore making his job twice as difficult as before. Eventually, he would come upon their tracks in the newly fallen snow, but that would be hours away, and by then the wolves may have traveled a far piece, having reached the treacherous slopes of the Bighorn Mountains. And if they reached the maze-like canyons and passes of the Bighorns, they could very well evade the hunter until they made it to the safety of the Rockies.

For the first time in his long career, Timber Gray felt a twinge of uncertainty. He had never doubted his ability as a hunter before, but that early morning he was having a few second thoughts. He had hunted the most dangerous game imaginable; grizzly, wildcat, wolf. The latter had always been his specialty, even though they were, by far, the most cunning and savage of the three. He reckoned he had bagged nearly five hundred of the beasts since coming west.

The thought of one man even hoping to track down and kill a pack of fifty wolves was flat-out suicidal. But then, deep down inside, wasn't that the reason he was hunting them in the first place? Ever since the slaughter of his family in the Tennessee mountains, hadn't he been hunting wolves simply for the chance of meeting one more cunning than all the others? Hadn't he braved the risks on the hope of finding that one wolf that would make it, unscathed, past his guns? Then it would be as it had been on the banks of Chestnut Creek, man against beast. And the stronger of the two would win, ending this tiresome quest for vengeance once and for all.

Timber pulled himself away from the blunt truth of his thoughts and uttered a soft curse beneath his breath. "You hunt wolves for the money," he grumbled to himself. "Not because of some damned death wish."

He gathered some wood and began to build a fire for his coffee. There would be a long way to ride before he reached the foothills of the Bighorn Mountains.

Chapter Ten

It wasn't long until he discovered an exodus of wolf tracks in the newly-fallen snow. They continued southward, through the vastly timbered foothills of the Bighorns. The wolfer tracked them through the following day, finding where the pack had split several times and regrouped. They seemed to be searching for something, perhaps a way to get to the other side of the mountain range. Whatever the reason for their quest, they were traveling with an uncanny intelligence that Timber Gray had never seen in a wolf pack before. Obviously their leader was a smart one. Perhaps smarter and more dangerous than any single wolf that he had ever set his sights on before.

There was something else that concerned him. For some time, Timber had been aware of travelers ahead of him. He had smelled the smoke of a campfire early that morning and come upon the deep rutted tracks of a wagon and shod horses weaving in and out of the foothills of the Bighorns. Like the wolves, it seemed that these travelers were attempting to find a clear way across the mountains, too.

It was nearing noon that day when he spotted the dark tint of woodsmoke against the heavy mat of stormclouds above. The hunter headed away from the wolf tracks he had been following, intending to find the wayward pilgrims and warn them of the marauding pack. But that was all, he swore to himself. After the friendly warning he would resume his task, hunting down the last of the wolves and trying to reach the town of Greybull before the worse of the blizzard hit the towering peaks. He was a professional tracker of dangerous game, not a guide and nursemaid for ignorant newcomers to this hard and hostile land.

"Hello the camp!" he called as he neared a heavy grove of fir trees. Someone answered, inviting him to come on in. The welcome eased Timber's mind somewhat and he returned his rifle to its saddle boot.

From the depth of the tracks, he had gathered that the wagon was pretty loaded down. He was right. It was an old prairie schooner, sagging with weight and age, its curved bows shrouded by a covering of patched canvas. The sideboards were adorned with supplies and farming implements lashed there with heavy rope. The four mule team was still harnessed to the iron tongue and looked to be of sturdy Missouri stock.

Timber Gray sat on his horse for a long moment, staring at the wagon. It was the type used when pioneers traveled in mass across the plains back in the 1840's. Truthfully, the last time he had actually seen one was after the Civil War, when thousands of Southerners traveled westward to escape the poverty and humiliation of a yankee-imposed Reconstruction.

Indeed, he was surprised to find such a wagon standing hub deep in snow among the mountains of Northern Wyoming. But what surprised him even more was the family who sat around a small cookfire to one side of the Conestoga.

The head of the family was a man of about thirty, tall and whipcord lean, dressed in the somber black vestments of a minister. His hair was thin and blond; his face hard and sour in expression. *Another Bible-thumping preacher*, noted Timber wearily. It wasn't that he disliked men of the cloth, it was just that they always ended up trying to convince him that his ways were leading him down the pathway to wickedness and sin. And that always seemed to stick in his craw.

The preacher's family looked cold and miserable. His wife was a wisp of a woman, dressed in a faded calico dress and bonnet. She was pretty in one way and downright plain in another. Her face was lined with fatigue and worry, wreathed in strands of mousy brown hair. The children stared at him with the same strange expression of relief as their mother did. The little girl couldn't have been over four years old, while the boy was perhaps nine or ten. They sat quietly, crouched near the fire, staring hungrily at johnnycake and beans; apparently the extent of their noontime meal.

Timber Gray swung down off his horse as the lean man approached him.

"Welcome, neighbor," he greeted, although there was a trace of disapproval and mistrust in his hard eyes. "My family and I were just sitting down to eat. Our meal is a meager one, but we would be pleased to have you join us."

Timber was reluctant to accept the man's offer, partly because he wanted to get back on the trail of the wolves and partly because he felt downright uncomfortable. It had been years since he had sat down to eat with decent folks like these and especially with a man of God. He wasn't sure if his manners were up to it or not.

"Well, now, I wouldn't want to intrude on you folks," he told them. The aroma of cornbread and white beans reached his cold-reddened nose and, he had to admit, it did smell mighty appetizing compared to his recent meals of beef jerky and hardtack.

"Nonsense," smiled the woman. She took a spare plate and began to ladle food onto its patterned surface. "Please, sit down."

"Much obliged," Timber said, nodding. He found a fallen place near the fire and sat down. The china plate felt warm as the woman handed it to him. Their eyes met for a second and, again, he noticed that puzzling look of relief, as if she were glad to see him, or anyone for that matter.

The wolfer was about to bring a forkful of beans to his mouth, when the preacher's withering glare stopped him. "Please, sir… let us give thanks to the Lord first."

"Sorry about that," mumbled Timber, returning the fork to his plate in embarrassment.

The reverend removed his black hat. The hunter did the same with his Stetson. It was during the man's long, rambling prayer that Timber noticed a disfiguring scar on the crown of the man's balding head. It was a deep mark, clearly the crescent shape of a horseshoe. He pulled his eyes from the scar just as the fellow ended his blessing with a hardy "Amen!" Then the curious indentation was hidden once again by the low, straight-brimmed hat.

"I am the Reverend Isaiah Cook," introduced the preacher around a mouthful of hot beans. "And this is my wife, Lenora, and my children, Paul and Sarah."

"Glad to make your acquaintance," Timber said. He tipped his hat politely at the nervous woman, then winked at the two young'uns. They giggled, until their father's steely eyes warned them back into obedient silence.

"What name do you go by, sir?"

"Timber Gray," answered the wolfer.

Isaiah stared at him for a long moment. "Oh, I see."

Timber was becoming increasingly uncomfortable under the disapproving study of the cassocked man. Maybe the preacher thought him to be an outlaw and his strange nickname nothing more than an alias. But he didn't care. He would tell them of the danger nearby, then ride on.

"I saw your tracks a few miles back and thought I'd stop and warn you that there's wolves in these mountains. A fair amount of wolves, and dangerous, too."

"Wolves!" exclaimed the woman, flustered at the frightening news. "Oh my!"

"Come now, Lenora!" Isaiah said sternly. "They too are creatures of God. If we pray for a safe journey across these mountains, I am sure that He will deliver us from the danger of the beasts."

"Praying is fine, I reckon," agreed Timber Gray. "But I'd still keep a couple of rifles loaded and ready just in case. Those mules there will be a mighty hard meal to pass up if that pack can't find anything else up here to satisfy their hunger."

Timber regretted having to be the bearer of bad tidings, especially since it was clearly beginning to upset the woman and her children. But the preacher seemed to blatantly dismiss his warning, piling his plate high and starting on a second helping of beans and cornbread.

"May I ask what you folks are doing out here in the middle of nowhere?"

"We are traveling to the town of North Fork," said the Reverend Cook. "The good citizens there need a minister for their town, so the family and I have left Minnesota to serve as missionaries of God's word in this sinful land."

Timber set his empty plate aside and took out the cloth bag of smoking tobacco. Again, he looked toward Lenora Cook and saw her eyes full of helplessness. They seemed to plead with him, as if saying "Please, talk some sense into him!" The children's faces held the same desperation, the little girl seeming close to tears. It was plain to see that they were all scared plumb to death of Isaiah and the potential danger he was dragging them into.

"What route are you taking to North Fork?" Timber asked the young preacher. "How are you gonna get over these mountains before the big snow hits?"

"That, sir, is no concern of yours," the reverend answered gruffly. "The Lord will provide us with a will and a way, and that shall take us to our destination safely."

"Please, Isaiah," said Lenora. "He's only trying to be helpful."

Isaiah Cook glared at his wife and, at first, Timber was afraid that the man might strike her. But his outrage was vented only with harsh words. "Still your tongue, woman! I'll not hear any disrespect from you!"

The woman shrank back, the moistness of tears welling in her eyes. The little girl joined in with frightened sobs of her own. The boy, Paul, stood stiffly beside the wagon's rear wheel, a look of pure hatred directed at his father's unsuspecting back.

Timber felt anger creep up on him, but he held his temper in check. "I reckon you could go through Burial Pass. It's about five miles south and it'll get you to Greybull before the blizzard gets here."

"Blizzard?" asked Lenora, her voice bewildered. "You mean there is more snow coming?"

"Afraid so, ma'am," said Timber, feeling like nothing but a doomsayer since he rode up.

Suddenly, the Reverend Cook stood up, as tall and unyielding as a black oak. His eyes burned angrily, almost insanely, at the bearded hunter. "I must ask you to leave now."

"Didn't mean to upset you or your family none," shrugged Timber. "Just trying to give you some friendly advice."

"I do not need the advice of a heathen gunfighter such as you!" declared Cook. His feverish eyes settled on the holstered .45 at Gray's hip, regarding it as though it was something obscene.

"What the hell are you talking about?" Timber felt the heat of rage prickling the nape of his neck.

Isaiah gestured his leather-bound Bible at the six-shooter. "You carry a gun freely and without shame. Guns are the fiery tools of Satan himself, spitting forth death and vileness in the robbery of hard-working folk and the drunken brawls of whorehouses and cowtown saloons. Any man who insists on carrying one is utterly lost. They, like you, will be damned to an everlasting hell!"

Timber Gray was on the point of slugging the man, when he remembered the cassock and Bible. He had never struck a man of God before, but was mighty tempted to do so at that moment. "Seems that I've outlived my welcome here," he said. He avoided looking at the frail woman and her two frightened youngsters as he turned and walked back to his horses.

Gray was untying the reigns from the trunk of a knotty pine, when he heard someone's footsteps in the snow behind him. He glanced over his shoulder to find Lenora Cook standing a few feet away, her lean arms crossed against the cold, her drawn face pale and etched with worry.

"Mr. Gray?"

"Yes, ma'am?" The wolfer turned back to his horse and fidgeted with the saddle straps, tightening those that seemed too loose, slackening those that seemed the least bit binding.

Lenora held out a small bag that jingled with the sound of coins. "I have thirty dollars in gold here, Mr. Gray. It may not be much to a man like you, but it is yours… if you'll get us safely to the nearest town."

Timber Gray tried not to look at the woman. "Keep your money, lady. I'm a wolf hunter, not a guide. Besides, your husband should've seen fit to hire one long before you got to territory this rough."

"We did hire a man to guide us, back in the Dakotas. His name was Joe Tully. We paid him fifty dollars, but he only led us to the Black Hills before he cut out one morning and left us to fend for ourselves. I reckon he'd had enough of my husband's preaching."

Timber nodded. He felt the same way. "I'm awful sorry, ma'am, but I've got wolves to find. The pass I mentioned is five miles or so due south from here. If you can beat the blizzard, you'll likely make it to Greybull safely."

He had put one foot in the stirrup and was about to swing into the saddle, when Lenora's frail hand clutched the sleeve of his coat. Her hold was tight and desperate, like the grasp of a drowning woman.

"If you don't help my children and I, Mr. Gray, we will all die out here in this godforsaken wilderness," Lenora said softly. "I believe you know that as well as I do."

Timber said nothing at first. There wasn't much that he could say. She and her children were in a bad way, stuck out in the middle of nowhere with very little food and practically no means of defending themselves. They were victims of Isaiah Cook's stupidity, at the mercy of a man who refused to carry a gun and knew nothing of the harsh land they now traveled.

The wolfer was torn between doing one of two things. He could do as he had for the past fifteen years, shunning humanity and minding his own business. Or he could do the decent thing. He didn't have to think twice to know that he really didn't have any choice in the matter.

"What about your husband?" he asked the woman. He looked toward the campfire where the good reverend knelt and prayed in a frighteningly loud voice, his stern face raised to the grayness of the heavens. The two children cringed from him and his fiery words, watching him as if he were a madman.

"This is a matter between you and I, Mr. Gray," said Lenora Cook. Her face had steeled itself with a calm born of inner strength. Obviously there was more backbone in this woman than Timber had first thought. "All that matters to me now is getting my babies to a town before they can freeze to death... or be set upon by wolves. As far as I'm concerned, my precious husband can stay out here in this frozen purgatory and take his chances. I won't continue to follow him and his stubborn blindness any longer."

The woman's words were harsh, but in Timber's mind they were also honest and admirable. "Keep your money till we get to Greybull," he told her.

"Then you'll help us get there safely?"

"Yes, ma'am. We'll head out now and most likely reach Burial Pass before dark. Wouldn't want to travel it by night, though. It's an awful treacherous canyon."

The woman gave Timber a rare smile, revealing a hint of the true beauty that hid beneath her drabness. "Then I will see to readying the wagon." She regarded the wolfer warmly. "God bless you, Mr. Gray."

The hunter blushed. "It'd be the first time in a long time, ma'am, but I thank you all the same."

Timber Gray turned back to his work and Lenora turned back to hers as well. The wolf hunter listened silently as the preacher argued with his wife over her hiring Gray as their guide. The minister grew more angry and indignant with each enraged word, but Lenora didn't give one inch. She stood up to her strong-headed husband for the first time in her life. And when the Reverend Isaiah Cook had finally ran out of steam and grown silent and brooding, Timber grinned and chuckled quietly to himself.

Chapter Eleven

The snowfall resumed by the time evening rolled around and they camped at the mouth of Burial Pass. It was not yet the blizzard they were expecting, but was much heavier than the light flurries that had powdered the mountain range on and off for the past few days.

Several yards outside the camp stretched the dark canyon of the pass. The walls of the ravine were extremely steep and sloped on each side, heaped with loose boulders and snow. Timber Gray knew the potential danger of that mountain thoroughfare. A single gunshot or even a loud yell could very well send an avalanche crashing down on unwary travelers. It had happened more than once in the years since Wyoming was first settled and the bodies of the unfortunate victims had lain beneath feet of rock and ice until spring thaw revealed their whereabouts. That was why it was known throughout the territory as Burial Pass.

As evening drew on into night, Timber and the Cook family sat around a blazing campfire. Their supper had been spare; the Cooks finishing off the leftover beans from earlier in the day, while Timber partook of his jerky and hardtack. Soon, Isaiah, who had been broodingly silent throughout that afternoon's journey, retired to the covered wagon. There he read his Bible by candlelight, leaving the others to pass the time in idle conversation.

"Your husband is mighty dedicated to his work," Timber said over a tin mug of steaming coffee.

Lenora's face was resentful. "Yes, much more dedicated to his work than to his own family, I'm afraid."

"Ma'am, you almost sound as though you disapprove of your husband's preaching."

"I am a religious woman, Mr. Gray," Lenora Cook told him. "I rejoice in hearing the word of the Lord preached by a capable minister. However, in my mind, Isaiah is not a rightful minister at all. He just took it upon himself to be one all of a sudden. He's not even a member of any particular church. Not Catholic, not Baptist, not Mormon."

"What about this church in North Fork? What denomination are they?"

Lenora was quiet for a long moment. Then she lifted troubled eyes to the bearded hunter. "There is no church waiting for us in North Fork, Mr. Gray. That is one of Isaiah's delusions... something his disturbed mind has conjured up to give his life a purpose. You see, my husband is... insane."

Timber was somewhat taken aback by the woman's bold statement. "Now, Mrs. Cook, your husband may be a little strong-headed in his beliefs, but I wouldn't peg him as being touched in the head."

Lenora Cook could see that her point wasn't getting through. "The man you know is not the man I married," she explained, keeping her voice low so Isaiah would not overhear. "When we were wed ten years ago, Isaiah was the best of providers, but he had his wild side. He wasn't above taking a drink every now and then and cussed up a storm when angered. But he was always good to the children and I. He never raised his hand to us and gave us a good home back in Minnesota.

"Isaiah was a farmer. He raised corn and wheat mostly, some tobacco. We lived happily for eight years. Paul was born, then precious Sarah. But it all changed one morning in the spring of '78. Isaiah was out plowing the northern pasture when one of the plowshares got caught in a tree root. Isaiah was trying to free it, when one of the mules got skittish. It kicked him squarely on the top of his head."

Timber recalled the shoe-shaped scar he had seen on the man's scalp. He could also tell that the memories were unpleasant, both for the woman and her children. "Ma'am, you needn't finish if you'd prefer not to."

"No, I want to tell you the rest... so that you'll understand." Lenora brushed a stray tear from one pallid cheek and continued. "For an entire week he lay in a state of unconsciousness, tossing and turning, talking out of his head. He finally came out of it on a Sunday morning and, from then on, we all knew he was not the same man. He grew brooding and despondent and took to reading the Bible. That in itself was strange, since Isaiah had never in any way been a religious man. At first I was pleased. Isaiah read the Good Book from cover to cover. But then it became an obsession. He would ride into town and preach in the square. Folks laughed at him, thought he was crazy. He even went to the saloon he once drank at and spouted sermons of hellfire and damnation. Soon, his old friends had enough and threw him out.

"That was two years ago, Mr. Gray. Since then we have been traveling constantly. Isaiah gave up farming and sold the land his father willed to him. He became a traveling preacher. It got to the point where only the most staunch of churchgoers would sit through one of his sermons. The children and I put up with it the best we could. Then he came up with this sudden exodus west to a place called North Fork. I saw no such letter inviting him to head that congregation and, in my heart, I believe there was no such invitation. I believe that my husband's sick and disillusioned mind urged him to take on such an impossible journey, perhaps to test his faltering faith.

"This has been a terrible ordeal for us, Mr. Gray. I thought we would be lost for sure... until you came along. And I truly thank God for that piece of luck."

The wolfer was flattered by the woman's confidence and was set at ease by her story. There had been several unanswered questions in Timber's mind up until that point and now, that they were out of the way, he could ride easier in the saddle, having a better idea of what to expect from this bogus reverend named Isaiah Cook.

"Don't you worry none, ma'am," Timber assured her. "We'll be heading down that pass tomorrow morn. Once we make it through, it'll be a downhill ride to the Bighorn River and Greybull. Why, I'd even lay a bet we might make it there before the worst of that snowstorm hits."

"I certainly hope so," Lenora said with a smile. Then her eyes turned serious again and, in a strange way, bitterly hard. "When we finally reach this town of Greybull, Mr. Gray, I shall not hesitate to take my children and leave Isaiah. Leave him to live his life and we to live ours. The further he drags us into the dangers of this hostile land, the more I realize that our lives are no longer as one, but are worlds apart."

Timber Gray said nothing. It was no place of his to agree or disagree with her decision. In fact, he knew deep down that her reasons were well justified. Crazy or not, Isaiah Cook was a dangerous man to travel with; a man blinded by the glory of God's word to the point of endangering his family in wilderness that was difficult for a seasoned westerner, let alone a greenhorn who absolutely refused to carry a gun.

———————

Later on, before everyone settled in for the night, Timber went out to fetch wood for the fire, enough to keep a steady blaze going throughout the twilight hours. Young Paul tagged along, carrying a kerosene lantern to help them through the dense shadows of the winter darkness.

There was a deadfall of jagged limbs and branches near the mouth of the pass. They headed for it, hoping to find some wood underneath dry enough for burning. As they stepped high through the sloping drifts, Timber felt the boy's eyes on him. After a few moments, the hunter decided it wasn't him that Paul was so interested in, but the holstered Colt .45 at his hip.

"Mr. Gray," the boy spoke up after a time. "Can I ask you something?"

"Sure, son," said Timber. He began to dig his way carefully through the skeletal remains of the deadfall. "What's on your mind?"

"Have you ever killed anyone?"

Timber wasn't really surprised by the question. Boys his age were usually fascinated with such things as guns and, yes, even death. The hunter had ridden through many a small town in Colorado and Arizona where the penalty for a heinous crime was public hanging. There he saw young boys standing for hours on end, watching an unfortunate outlaw dangle and swing in the breeze. He didn't rightly see the fascination as being healthy, not for young'uns who should be shooting marbles or running barrel hoops instead. But curiosity was just a part of growing up and death was an inevitable part of that curiosity.

The hunter tossed a few jagged limbs into the snow and regarded the nine-year-old. "Now, I ain't gonna lie to you, Paul. I have killed a few men in my time... but only when I had to." His mind conjured up images of the men who had fallen before his gun. Two in the War Between the States and one in Abilene, Kansas a few years back. The latter had been a touchy gambler with a fancy, pearl-handled gun and mighty little luck to go with it.

Paul Cook's eyes widened with excitement. "Did you shoot them with that gun right there?"

"No," chuckled Timber. He tossed a few more branches onto the pile. "Ain't had a chance to shoot much of nothing with this hogleg yet."

The boy nodded, frowning in apparent disappointment. Then suddenly another grisly thought popped into mind. "When we passed through Deadwood in the Dakotas, there were two men laid out in the undertaker's window. They'd faced each other in a gunfight and shot each other stone-cold dead. They got each other square through the heart. Now, ain't that something?"

"I reckon so," replied Timber. The boy's enthusiasm was making him feel awkward now. "But you shouldn't be talking over such things with a stranger, boy. Seems like your pa should tell you what you want to know about death."

Paul frowned again. "Nah, he only talks about what it'll be like after you die. You know, a weeping and wailing and a gnashing of teeth. Do you think that's how it's going to be when you die, Mr. Gray?"

The hunter didn't know quite what to say. "I don't rightly know how it'll be, Paul. But I'm hoping it'll turn out a sight better than that."

Timber Gray walked around to the other side of the deadfall. Paul followed, holding the lantern ahead of him. As he glanced off down the pass they would be traveling the next day, Timber noticed a disturbance in the snow. "Bring the light closer," he told the boy. Slipping the thong off the hammer of his sidearm, he and Paul walked toward the swathe of churned snow.

The dark indentations were wolf tracks. From the vast number of them, it looked to be the pack he was after. The tracks were about half a day old. The snow had hardened, leaving a crust of solid ice around each print. Timber looked down the narrow channel of Burial Pass where the tracks disappeared into the night. The sudden realization that they were so near sent a chill down the wolfer's spine.

"Let's get on back to the wagon," he told the boy. They were turning to leave, when the yellow glow of the lamp caught a separate set of tracks apart from the others. "Wait just a minute," he said and knelt to examine them.

"Funny looking tracks," commented Paul.

He was right. They were strangely different from the others, although they were also made by a wolf. They were slightly larger, obviously those of the white-furred leader that Gray had seen the day he had sniped the pack from the rocky ridge. But the size was not the cause of his sudden interest. It was the right front paw print—missing all the toes and half the foot—that brought a smile of dawning revelation.

"Well, I'll be damned," he cursed softly. "Old Cripplefoot."

Paul crouched beside the bearded man, providing lamplight and feeling a little scared over their sudden discovery. "Who's Old Cripplefoot?"

Timber Gray didn't answer. He only stared at the mismatched tracks with a sensation of excited satisfaction welling up inside him. Yes, he was sure of it. The tracks belonged to the wolf all right.

Old Cripplefoot was something of a legend in the Rockies. The renegade wolf had first been encountered back in the 1840's, when buckskinned mountain men trapped the cold water streams for beaver. It was said that the wolf lost half his front paw to a bear trap and, ever since then, had haunted the settlers of the Continental Divide with his cunning and savagery. Over twenty-five deaths had been blamed on Old Cripplefoot and men had gone after him with a vengeance many times, determined to hunt him down and make a trophy of his hide. But no one had ever been that lucky. Dozens had claimed point-blank shots at the elusive wolf, but the animal had escaped in every instance. The Blackfoot and Sioux considered him a bad spirit, for they too had hunted him unsuccessfully, chasing him into dead-end canyons only to find their prey gone, as if his very being had been spirited away by the wind.

Timber scoffed at the tales of a ghostly wolf. He knew Old Cripplefoot was as real as any other wolf. In fact, he probably knew the wolf better than any other hunter alive. Gray had tracked the animal twice before. The first time had been in the San Juans of southern Colorado, the second in the Bitterroot Mountains near Lochsa River. Both hunts had been futile, leaving Timber with a feeling of frustrated defeat and, oddly enough, a grudging respect for the old wolf. To put it simply, Cripplefoot was the cleverest and most elusive critter that Gray had ever set his sights on.

The hunter stood in the cold darkness, a frigid northerner ruffling his clothing and whipping around the crown of his silverbelly hat. His dark gray eyes were mere slits as he stared down the pass, perhaps searching for the darting shadows of wolves on the prowl. Having Old Cripplefoot as a leader made any wolf pack twice as dangerous as before, especially one as large as this one. And he would sure hate to meet up with them in the narrow confines of Burial Pass, unable to fire his gun in the fear of bringing tons of snow and rock down upon their heads.

"I think it'd be best not to say anything about this to your ma and pa," he suggested, clapping a friendly hand on the boy's quivering shoulder. "No need to upset them none."

"All right," agreed Paul.

They went back to work, gathering enough dry kindling to last the night. As they headed back for camp, Paul carrying the lantern while Timber followed with an armload of branches, the wolf hunter's thoughts were occupied with Old Cripplefoot. The wolf had always been a sore spot with him. In fact, he had even gotten into several barroom brawls because some drunken cowpoke had brought up Timber's failure to catch him.

But now he had another chance at the 'ghost wolf'. And he swore to God that, this time, the aim of his big Sharps 50-caliber would draw blood.

Fatal blood.

Chapter Twelve

The only wolf they found in the narrow stretch of Burial Pass was a dead one.

The she-wolf had obviously crossed some of the other pack members, over food or perhaps a mate. She had fought savagely, but the sheer number of the others had proven no contest. They had left her there, eager to move onward down the pass to the far side of the mountains. The animal's body was cold when Timber Gray came upon it a few hours later, but not frozen. He had no trouble skinning her and lashing her bloodstained hide to the pack horse along with the others.

From there on out, the riding went smoothly. There was no more sign of wolves or other dangerous game, except for the recent tracks of the marauding pack. The Reverend Cook had regained his old fire and constantly spouted scripture as they moved onward. However, the preacher's sermons were more subdued in their fury than they had been before. Timber Gray mostly attributed it to the fear of an avalanche. The pastor was aware that his righteous bellowing could very well bring disaster crashing down upon their heads. Timber was grateful for his restraint, since any loud noise could send a deadly ricochet of echoes bouncing off the steep, snow-laden walls and bring instant, crushing death.

For a while, the wolfer actually thought they would make it through the treacherous mountain pass without incident. But as the day drew on and only a few miles lay between them and the western foothills, they began to hear the distant murmur of voices and the snow-muffled footfalls of horses. The Cook family seemed anxious to meet the approaching riders, perhaps because they had encountered so few people since leaving the Dakotas. But Timber Gray's feelings led more to suspicion. Something told him that these men could prove to be trouble if given half the chance.

As the sounds grew nearer, Timber stopped his black gelding and motioned for Isaiah to rein the wagon's mule team to a halt. The two pack horses did likewise, a steady drift of frozen breath wafting from their flared nostrils.

"Reverend," Timber said in a low voice. "I'd appreciate it if you'd keep quiet and let me do the talking here. There are some mean ones in these mountains who don't take kindly to newcomers. Don't know if these men are like that, but I don't aim to take any chances, not in this canyon."

"Now, see here, Mr. Gray," protested Isaiah Cook. "I have as much right to converse with these gentlemen as you do. What if they are in need of spiritual guidance? Should I just turn them away?"

The voices became clearer as the riders neared a bend up ahead. The snicker of dirty laughter and cussing drifted down the length of Burial Pass. Timber looked the young minister squarely in the eye. "Preacher, the only spirits them fellas are interested in are what come out of a whiskey bottle. If you start shooting off your mouth and calling them a pack of no-account sinners, I'm afraid they'll give us some real trouble."

"Please, Isaiah," said Lenora, putting a firm hand on her husband's   arm. "Let Mr. Gray handle this. He knows these people better than we." The woman sat on the seat of the wagon, while the two children napped in the rear.

"Very well," grumbled Isaiah, but his venomous glare told Timber that he was far from being satisfied.

Timber Gray sat in the saddle and looked toward the turn in the pass. As an afterthought, he shucked his Winchester from its boot, levered a cartridge into the breach, and laid the rifle easily across his knees. Firing a shot in this canyon was the last thing in the world he wanted to do. But if these men came upon them intending to start trouble, then the only thing he could do was oblige them and hope that the walls didn't come tumbling down around their heads.

Five men on lean mountain horses appeared around the bend and sauntered slowly toward them. Two men looked to be brothers, each wearing overcoats and gray derby hats. One carried a shotgun, the other a Winchester carbine. Another rider was a bear of a man in a tall-crowned hat, bearded and scarred deeply down one side of his ruddy face. A tarnished cavalry sword hung from his saddle horn, along with other weapons. Next to him rode a youngster of about eighteen. He was clean-shaven, all decked out in black, and wore a fancy, ivory-handled Colt tied down to his right thigh. The kid looked like hair-triggered trouble in a pint-sized package; someone who was just itching to show off his prowess with a shooting iron.

The fifth man, the leader of the ragged bunch, was a lean man in an old gray frockcoat and a low black hat. His ugly face was dirty and bristled, his mouth sparkling with twenty dollars worth of gold dental work, and his eyes were full of pure meanness. A sawed-off ten-gauge hung from his saddle, but that was not the weapon that caught Timber's attention. It was a brace of pistols belted around the leader's waist that stood out; a couple of old .44 Dragoons that had been converted to fire metallic cartridges.

Timber Gray recognized a couple of the men immediately. The leader was Elijah Cox and the bearded one was his right-hand man, Avery Gimble. He couldn't place the two brothers, as well as the kid with the fifty dollar gun. But they were all plainly cut of the same cloth. Bounty hunters. Timber could tell one a mile away. They always exuded a somber feeling of violent death, not only to those they hunted, but to decent folks as well. From what Timber had heard, Elijah Cox was the best of his profession. He had ridden with Quantrill as a guerilla fighter back during the war and, afterwards, had found profit in hunting down outlaws for gold. Bringing them "back alive" held no meaning for Cox or the men he rode with. The fugitives Cox went after always came back tied over a saddle, a bullet hole through their head or torso and a wanted poster stuck in their mouth.

The five urged their mounts forward, spreading out as they reached the wagon. Elijah rode up to Timber Gray with Gimble and the kid to his right and left. The two brothers halted their horses on the far side of the wagon, nearly out of the wolfer's sight. Timber didn't like that one bit.

"Howdy," greeted Elijah, displaying a grin of yellow gold. "You folks lost? Ain't normal for someone to be traveling these mountains all loaded down with a wagon and all. And with heavy snow on its way, too."

Timber Gray regarded the bounty hunter with a cool stare. "Ain't lost. Just trying to get to Greybull before the worst of the storm hits." The wolfer eyed each man, then returned his eyes to the leader. "Are you boys up here looking for someone?"

Elijah Cox chuckled. "I reckon you know of us and our business then," he said. "Yeah, we're after a man, all right. Been tracking him all the way from Colorado for the past few weeks. As slippery a critter as we've gone after, too." Cox fumbled through an inner pocket of his duster and unfolded a crumpled broadsheet. He handed it to the wolfer. "Wonder if you've seen him in these parts?"

Timber Gray took the poster and looked it over. WANTED—LUKE BELL FOR THE ROBBERY & MURDER OF MAYOR DANIEL SPENCER OF DURANGO, COLORADO. $1,000 REWARD.

Below the bold lettering was a crudely drawn sketch of a black man in his late twenties. His hair was short-cropped, his eyes and teeth almost comically white in contrast to his soot-black face. Whoever had drawn the picture had let his prejudice against the Negro race bleed through, loud and clear.

"Can't say that I have," said Timber with a shrug. He held the poster so Isaiah Cook and his wife could see it. "Have either of you seen this man?" They shook their heads negatively and remained silent.

Elijah grinned sheepishly and returned the poster to his coat pocket. "Just ain't having a lick of luck a'tall today. Ain't that right, boys?" The others grumbled in lackluster reply.

Avery Gimble walked his horse closer. He studied the wolf pelts on the pack horse, then eyed Timber with interest. "Hey, ain't you that wolf hunter?" he asked in a gravely voice. "That fella called Timber Gray?"

The wolfer said that he was.

"Yeah, that's right!" proclaimed Elijah. "I saw you once in Green River City. You came riding through town with the biggest damned bear I ever did see, lashed to two horses. Remember that?"

Indeed, Timber did remember the grizzly he had taken November of last year down in the Bishop Mountains of southern Wyoming. The bear had been a nasty one. He had

71

happened upon his cave by accident and found it littered with all manner of bones, those of a man included. Timber's bones might have joined them if he hadn't turned in time and put a .50 slug through the grizzly's brain pan as it was coming for him.

"Looks like we're almost in the same profession, Mr. Gray," ventured Cox, scratching his scraggly whiskers. "You know... hunting for bounty and all."

"Except there's a difference," replied Gray. "At least I sleep well at night, knowing my victims are killers. You never really know whether the men you bushwhacked were innocent or guilty."

Elijah Cox's golden grin faded. His true colors showed as his eyes glowered coldly at the wolfer, smoldering with an ugly meanness. "Mister, you just went down a notch or two in my good graces."

Timber Gray knew he should have let it go at that, but he just couldn't seem to pass up the urge. "You've been at the bottom of mine from the very start," he said. It slowly began to dawn on him exactly how dangerous it was to needle this man. Was it the death wish again, creeping up and pushing him toward a stand-off that would likely end up killing them all?

Their mutual bad feelings might have led to trouble, if something hadn't happened to draw their attention. That something turned out to be the boy in black. He had trotted his dark horse to the wagon and was looking it over suspiciously. "Don't you think we oughta check this wagon, Elijah? They might be hiding Bell, trying to get him down to Greybull past us."

Cox forgot his beef with Timber for the time being. He rode past the wolfer, toward the side of the prairie schooner. He leaned over in his saddle and put his ear to the wall of bowed canvas. "You just might be right, Jess. I hear somebody breathing inside." He turned and eyed Timber and the couple on the wagon seat. "Now, you good folks ain't hiding someone from us, are you?"

"There's no one back there but a couple of young'uns," said Timber Gray. He felt his temper heating at the thought of them scaring Paul and Sarah needlessly. "They're getting some rest. No need to upset them none."

The boy named Jess sneered at the wolfer and began to swing down off his horse. "Scaring young'uns ain't something I lose much sleep over."

"I wouldn't do that if I was you."

The kid stood there by his horse and stared up at the bearded hunter, peeved at his warning. It was then that he noticed the Winchester lying across Timber's lap, the muzzle directed squarely at his chest.

"You pointing that thing at me?" Jess hissed, his face growing pale with anger.

"What... *this*?" asked Timber Gray, looking down at the cocked rifle. His eyes were full of innocence, but his finger never left the trigger.

"I'm not one for playing games, mister," said the boy. "That's why I'm ending it right here and now." He slipped the thong off his Colt and slowly began to draw his gun of ivory and etched silver.

Timber looked over to where Elijah Cox still sat on his horse. "Are you gonna tell this hotheaded fool where we are, before he gets us all killed?"

The bounty hunter glared at Gray, then nodded. "Put the gun away, Jess."

The kid looked indignant. "The hell I will!"

"I said put it away... now!"

Bewildered, Jess let the gun slip back into its low-slung holster. "But why, Elijah? Why didn't you let me plug this old buzzard?"

"Cause this is Burial Pass we're in, you piss-ant!" Cox snapped. "You fire a gun in this canyon and we'd all be under a trainload of snow till spring!"

Jess was shocked by the sobering explanation. He turned his eyes to the snowy walls of the pass and stared at them for a long time.

At that moment, Paul and Sarah climbed out of the rear of the wagon and ran to join their parents on the front seat.

"Reckon you weren't lying to us after all," said Elijah, flashing another lopsided grin.

"I think we'd best be on our way," Timber replied, his expression as cold as stone. "And I know you'll be wanting to get back to tracking that man Bell."

"Come on, boys," called Cox. He reined his horse toward the eastern end of the pass. "We've wasted too much time here already."

Jess scowled at the wolf hunter and swung back atop his horse. He patted his holstered Colt with a gloved hand. "I'll be saving one for you, old man," he sneered. "Someday we'll cross paths again and it won't be in some damned avalanche pass."

"You're not long for this country, boy," Timber told him flatly. "Not with that kind of attitude."

The kid was about to say something else, when Elijah Cox rode up and slapped the rump of the boy's horse. "Get going, Jess," he said, sending the horse at a steady gallop down the canyon. Then Cox turned in his saddle and regarded Gray. "You may not like our kind of hunting, mister, but don't go badmouthing it none. We do our killing nice and legal like, but sometimes I do get the old urge to drill a man for the pure fun of it. And, Mr. Timber Gray, you're coming mighty close to being that unfortunate soul."

Then, with an ugly, gold-studded grin, he rode off down the pass to join the others. Timber Gray sat there for a long moment, letting his anger die down before heading onward himself. He knew he had just made a couple of very dangerous enemies that day. Men who killed for a living and relished in the feel of it. Timber had encountered their kind before, promising to collect on unfinished grudges. In every case, he had never laid eyes on them again afterwards.

But, somehow, Timber Gray knew that wouldn't be the case with Elijah Cox and his gang.

Chapter Thirteen

The following morning brought a steady snow and an icy wind from the north. They had cleared Burial Pass late last evening and had set up camp a mile or so into the foothills. With each passing hour, the temperature dropped and the northern gale blew more and more snow across the mountains toward the town of Greybull.

Timber Gray sat in a small lean-to of heavy pine boughs, sewing up an embarrassing rip in the seat of a pair of faded longhandles. The Cook family had settled their wagon and team across the clearing from him. His coal black gelding was hitched to a towering blue spruce between the two camps, along with the two pack horses.

After fussing over the threadbare drawers for a while, Gray glanced up to see little Sarah standing before him. Her face was creased with sadness and she appeared almost on the verge of tears.

Timber set his mending aside. "Now, whatever is the matter, Miss Sarah?" he asked the four-year-old. "You don't look like you're none too happy."

"Could you fix my dolly, Mr. Gray?" she sniffled. Sarah held out her china doll. Its white porcelain head had separated from the rag body. "Mama's too busy cooking breakfast."

The bearded wolfer smiled at the fair-haired youngster. "I'll surely see what I can do, honey."

Sarah sat on the old Indian blanket beside him. Taking the needle and thread from his hopelessly split ridgerunners, Timber began to meticulously reattach the doll's head to its body.

Timber Gray winked at little Sarah and received a giggle of affection in return. He had been guiding the Cook family for a couple of days now and already the children had taken to him as though he was a long, lost uncle. The hunter had been apprehensive at first, for it had been a long time since he had lived among the laughter and playfulness of young'uns. But, soon, his hardened heart had warmed up to Paul and Sarah. He also held high regards for their mother, her being as brave and strong-willed a woman as he had ever met. The only one in the Cook clan that Timber was still uncertain of was the Reverend Isaiah. Something about the man's ways just didn't set well with the wolf hunter.

As he tightened the last stitch in the china doll's neck, Timber glanced through the light flurry of January snowflakes, toward the wagon and the large cookfire blazing near its rear gate. Lenora was preparing the morning meal, while Isaiah fed the mules their share of oats. But someone was missing. Paul Cook was nowhere to be seen.

"Where's your brother, Miss Sarah?" he asked, handing the doll back to her.

"Papa sent him over the hill to fetch some water," Sarah replied, more occupied with her repaired toy than Timber's question.

"Alone?"

"Uh-huh. He didn't wanna go by himself, but Papa made him."

Timber Gray felt his dislike for the preacher come to a boil again. He was standing up, ready to give Isaiah hell for sending the boy to the stream alone, when a crash of tin pans sounded from the campfire. Timber looked over to see Lenora standing there, her thin hands to her face and her mouth widened in a silent scream. The hunter followed her frantic eyes to where they stared in horror.

Paul was running down a distant hillside as fast as his legs would carry him, the water bucket discarded and forgotten. His frightened cries filled Timber's ears, chilling his heart with terror. Over the boy's yells there came another sound; a sound that Gray was painfully familiar with. The snapping and snarling of hungry wolves, six of which were gaining on Paul Cook at that very moment.

Timber's eyes flashed to where his rifles were booted on his horse, a good fifteen feet away. Lenora had regained her senses and she also spotted the weapons jutting invitingly into the winter air. Running to the spruce, she pulled the Winchester from its sheath and held it out to her husband.

"Shoot them, Isaiah!" she cried. "For heaven's sake, shoot them before they kill our son!"

The Reverend stared at her and the rifle with an expression of pure disgust. "I will not! I'll not lay a hand on that instrument of Satan!"

"You must!" Lenora wailed. "Confound you, Isaiah! You've got to do something!" She shoved the repeater toward her husband.

But the preacher would have none of it. He backhanded her viciously, sending her and the rifle into the snow. "You will burn in Hell for that, woman!" he spat. Then he dropped to his knees and, clutching his worn Bible, began to pray at the top of his lungs.

Timber ran toward the horses, his eyes glued to the snow-crusted hillside a hundred yards away. The boy was losing his speed, out of breath and stumbling through the heavy snow. The wolves, however, were gaining. They had caught scent of the child's fear and were moving in for the kill. It wouldn't be long before they dragged their prey off balance and stained the virgin snow with his blood.

The wolfer leaped for the fallen rifle, rolled, and came up in a crouch, the Winchester already cocked and ready. He picked out the wolf closest to the boy, steadied his aim, and fired. The first slug drilled the wolf squarely in the snout, burrowing clear to the base of its brain. The animal's legs collapsed beneath it and it dropped dead in its tracks.

The .44-40 shucked its fired brass from the breach and chambered another round as Timber worked the lever. Once again the rifle cracked, then a third time. Two wolves collided with each other, their innards speared by well-placed lead.

"Three more!" gritted the hunter between clenched teeth. "Lord, just give me three more, that's all I ask!"

He shifted his barrel a fraction and fired again. A she-wolf spun head over tail, her skull opened up just below the left ear. Timber pulled back on the trigger again, his hand having worked the lever automatically. The fifth wolf continued to run, a long bloody furrow cut across its hindquarters. The next bullet did not miss its mark, though. It caught the beast squarely in the brisket.

One wolf left. It couldn't have been more than a yard behind the boy, its slavering jaws snapping in anticipation, its eyes crazed with bloodlust. Gray hesitated in firing. They were so close to each other now that the wolfer was afraid he might miss his aim and hit the boy. But there was no other choice to be made. He had to fire. The rifle slapped against his shoulder with the recoil of the next shot. The bullet missed its target, kicking up snow between the wolf's swift legs.

"Damn!" Timber Gray cussed and readied the Winchester for one last shot. He held his breath and, for a split second, the rifle barrel stopped its trembling and froze dead center on the animal. "Got you," said Timber. He eased back smoothly on the trigger.

Paul Cook fell just as the slug hit the wolf right between the eyes. The beast rolled completely over the frightened boy with the force of its momentum. It flipped down the snowy slope until finally stopping with a sickening thud against the trunk of a huge oak. Paul got shakily to his feet, splattered with the wolf's blood, and ran straight into his mother's outstretched arms.

"Thank you, Mr. Gray!" wept Lenora, clutching her son close. "You saved him. You saved my boy's life."

Timber said nothing. He slid the rifle back into its scabbard and walked over to where the preacher still knelt in the frigid snow. He stood there, glaring at Isaiah Cook until he had said his closing "Amen!" and began to stand up. Then Timber hauled back and punched the good reverend right in the teeth.

Isaiah stumbled backwards and fell on his back beside the roaring fire. He looked up at the bearded hunter in bewilderment, his lip split and his mouth smeared with blood. "You struck a man of God!" he bellowed.

"No!" Timber told him, enraged. "I struck a crazy fool who'll not raise a finger to protect his own family. Well, you listen to me, preacherman, and listen good. Your mule-headedness ends right here! The next time trouble shows itself, you'd best be ready to take up a gun. Cause, if you don't, I swear I'll shoot you myself and leave you as food for the buzzards!"

The hunter saw fear in the man's eyes and knew that he had succeeded in shocking him back into reality, at least for the time being. Timber hoped it would last for a while, because the next time the wolves set upon them, there was sure to be much more than six. And he would need all the help he could get, even if it meant tying a gun in the preacher's hand.

"I reckon I'd better get on up the hill and skin out those wolves," he said, looking toward Lenora Cook. She stood beside the campfire, holding both her youngsters to her skirt. "Maybe you should go on and finish the breakfast, ma'am. We'll be on our way in an hour or so."

"All right," agreed Lenora. She looked down at her bleeding husband and then back at the wolfer. A strange smile of cold satisfaction crossed her lips briefly, then vanished as she turned back to the cookfire.

Timber Gray drew his bone-handled knife from its belt sheath. He untied the pack horse with the hides lashed across its back and started across the clearing to the foot of the bloodstained hill. A moment later, Paul Cook's voice called out from behind him.

"Mr. Gray?"

Timber glanced around. "Yes, boy?"

"Mr. Gray… can I come with you?"

Lenora put a trembling hand on her son's shoulder. "Maybe you shouldn't, Paul."

"No, ma'am, it's okay," Timber replied, regarding the boy with deep admiration. It seemed to him that Paul had twice as much backbone than his old man did. "There's nothing up there that can hurt him now."

The woman nodded in understanding and went back to her chores. Paul ran to the wolf hunter, his youthful face still pale and frightened, but his eyes steeled with determination.

No words were exchanged as they went up the snowy hillside together.

Chapter Fourteen

Standing atop a snowy ridge, Timber Gray trained his field glasses on the distant town of Greybull. A few kerosene-lit windows could be seen through the blowing snow, but soon the buildings would grow dark as the townspeople settled in for the night. There was a mile or two of dense forest between the Wyoming settlement and the clearing where Gray and the Cooks had made their camp. If there had been a moon that night, the wolfer might have seen the churning waters where the Bighorn and Greybull rivers forked. But the valley below was as black as the depths of a Kentucky coalmine, the blusterous sky hanging heavy with thick stormclouds. The blizzard would reach the western side of the mountain before morning and cover the sloping countryside with a blanket of snow that would lie dormant until spring.

The wolf hunter pulled the fleeced collar of his sheepskin coat around his whiskered face and, with his .44-40 under his arm, started down the rocky ridge. As he neared the blazing fire, Timber could not help but feel spooked for some reason. Things had gone smoothly following the incident with the six wolves. According to his figuring, the pack must number close to thirty-two now, eighteen down from their original strength, but still a formidable bunch.

Through the increasing snowfall, Timber and the greenhorn family had made their way through the winding foothills. By afternoon, they had happened upon an abandoned stage road and had followed its course westward until dark. Timber had hoped to reach Greybull by nightfall, but the increasing intensity of the snowstorm had forced them to stop and make camp.

He walked silently down the steep hillside, ducking through pines and firs, their needled boughs heavy with mats of accumulated snow. The bright glow of the fire could be seen just ahead. As Timber made his way to the safety of the camp, he turned suspicious eyes toward the blackness beyond the sifting snow. The uneasy feeling simply would not desert him. Ever since they had left the hillside of Paul's terrified run, the hunter had sensed the wolves just out of sight. He knew they were there in the dense woods at the side of the stage road, for he had been stalked before and knew the feeling. He would catch a quick flash of motion out of the corner of his eye, but by the time he turned, there would only be empty forest. Still, he could feel their eyes upon him; angry eyes... hungry eyes, glaring at the man who had vowed to have their hides. He sensed those burning eyes now, as he reached the boundary of their roadside camp. He was not the only one. The mules and horses also seemed nervous, aware that other animals were lurking nearby. Deadly animals.

"Greybull is just over the rise there," Timber told them as he passed the tethered horses and approached the warmth of the fire.

Lenora Cook and her children sat huddled in blankets on one side of the blaze. Isaiah Cook was nowhere to be seen. The slight illumination of a coal oil lamp through the wagon's canvas top told Timber that the reverend was probably meditating over the Gospels. The preacher had kept clear of them since the wolfer had nearly knocked his teeth down his throat earlier that day.

"Here, have some coffee," smiled Lenora, filling his tin mug with the steaming brew.

Gray took a seat on a frosty boulder and gratefully accepted the hot cup. "Much obliged, ma'am."

"Tell us another story, Mr. Gray," urged little Sarah.

"Yeah," said Paul, the boy's face glowing with anticipation. "Tell us another story about the wolves."

Timber Gray had been spinning some yarns and tall tales earlier on in the evening, some about people he had met, some about the hunts he had been on since coming west. "I don't know if I ought to," he told them now. "Your ma here might not like me telling you such stories."

Lenora's frown of disapproval melted into a soft smile. "Oh, maybe just one more. Then it's off to bed with the both of you. We'll be riding into town in the morning and I'll not have a couple of sleepy-heads on my hands."

"Tell us!" piped the youngsters. "Tell us another one!"

"All right," agreed Timber, taking another sip from his mug and then balancing it on his knee. "Seems I once heard tell of a mountain man who lived in the Rockies some twenty years back. His name was Gabriel Bass and folks said he was a grizzly of a man with a long red beard and dressed all in buckskin. He carried a knife near as long as his leg and a muzzleloading Hawken with twenty brass studs on the stock, one for each injun he'd shot there in the mountains.

"Well, now, one day ol' Bass went hunting up in the Great Divide with a friend of his by the name of Mexicany Max. They'd gotten them a couple of big elk and were heading back for their cabin, when they looked around and what do you think they spotted? Why, it was a dozen timber wolves as hungry as could be! Bass cut an elk loose off his horse and they swallowed it whole, horns and all. But they were still hungry and licking their chops. Another mile passed, then he threw down the other elk and those wolves gulped that one down, too.

"Ol' Gabe Bass and Mexicany Max, they left their horses behind and made a run for it. Well, the wolves, they swallowed them horses and kept right on a-coming. Bass said to his partner that he'd rest and shoot a wolf and then run while Max was resting and shooting. So they did, going down the mountainside like that. Bass would shoot one and the wolf behind it would swallow it down. Then Max would shoot and another wolf would end up in its partner's hungry belly."

Paul and Sarah gasped in bewilderment. Their mother shook her head and began cleaning up the supper dishes, her eyes gleaming with amusement.

"It seems that they kept it up, loading and shooting, till they'd shot eleven of the varmints, all of which had been eaten by the one after it. Then Mexicany Max yelled "Good God Almighty, Gabe, look-a-there!" Ol' Bass looked behind him and there, right on their tails, was the biggest danged wolf they'd ever laid eyeballs on. Why, he was as big as a buffalo!"

"So what happened?" asked Paul urgently, not wanting to miss a single word.

"Well, Gabriel Bass drew his old Arkansas toothpick, turned on the wolf, and stuck it in his belly. Then he cut it open and let them two horses out. After that, he and Max lashed the two elks back on the horses, skinned all twelve wolves, one outta the other, and rode on to the cabin like they'd first intended."

Paul Cook bought the tall tale for a moment more, then frowned in suspicion. "You've been funning us all along, haven't you, Mr. Gray?"

The wolfer replied with a hearty laugh and the two children reddened with embarrassment, feeling downright foolish. Lenora laughed also and Timber was startled by the gentle sound of her voice. He winked across the fire at her and was pleased when she returned his gesture with a warm smile.

"All right, that's enough for tonight," said Lenora, herding her children off to bed. "Any more wolf stories and you'll be having nightmares."

"Good night, Mr. Gray," called Paul and Sarah as they climbed into the back of the wagon.

"Sleep tight, young'uns," the man replied. He lifted the coffee pot and poured the rest, grounds and all, into his tarnished cup. He heard the faint sounds of their prayers, then looked up to see Lenora Cook. She sat down across the fire from him.

They sat in awkward silence for a time, then Timber broke it with a question he knew he really had no business asking. "Ma'am, you told me before that you intended to leave your husband when we reach Greybull. Are you still aiming to do that?"

"After the way he acted this morning when those wolves were after Paul? I should say so, and we'll all be better off for it."

Gray frowned and was suddenly aware of his concern for the woman. It had been a long time since the bearded hunter had felt that way toward a female. Not since Rebecca.

"But what will you do?" he asked her. "Where will you go?"

"Back to Minnesota, I suppose," she told him. "I reckon I'll find a job, perhaps in a dress shop. I used to be a pretty good

87

seamstress before I married Isaiah. We'll manage, the children and I. We'll build us a new life, a new home."

They returned to their silence. Only the whistling of the wind and the crackle of the fire could be heard. Then Lenora stared at the bearded man for a long moment. "Mr. Gray... do you have a home to go to after all this is over?"

Timber Gray felt a nagging sadness tug at his innards, but didn't let it show. "My home is out here in the wilderness, ma'am. The mountains, the plains, the desert... any place I lay my head. Some folks say I live like the critters I hunt; on the move with no roots to tie me down."

"But no man should live in such a manner," said Lenora. "A man should have some loved ones, a family who can depend on him and make him feel wanted. Don't you have any such kin, Mr. Gray?"

"None that I know of since I left Tennessee."

"No wife?" persisted the woman. "No children to carry on their father's name?"

"No, ma'am," replied the hunter, his voice strained with indifference. "Not anymore."

Lenora could see that the quiet man did not want to discuss his past and she did not bother to pursue it any further. With a tired sigh, she stood and turned toward the wagon. "I believe I'll turn in now. We have much to do tomorrow."

Timber Gray nodded solemnly and fished the tobacco pouch from his shirt pocket. "You go ahead, ma'am. I'll throw some more wood on the fire and turn in myself directly."

She walked a couple of steps, then stopped. "You know, you make me feel like an old maiden aunt calling me ma'am like that," she smiled shyly. "You may call me Lenora, if you'd like."

Gray appreciated the thought. "I'd like that... Lenora. And you can just call me Timber from here on out."

Lenora Cook wrinkled her nose at the nickname. "Surely you weren't born with such a name. What is your Christian name?"

"It's Jefferson," he replied after a moment. "Haven't used it in so long that I nearly forgot what it was."

"Well, good night, Jefferson." Then she was in the wagon, away from the bite of the wind, if not the frigid cold itself.

Timber Gray rolled himself a cigarette and smoked for a while, his mind in deep thought. He was a little peeved at himself for avoiding Lenora's innocent questions and acting like a bitter shell of a man. He had wanted to tell her of his life; of the little log cabin in the Smokies. He had wanted to tell her of Rebecca and Todd and the day on Chestnut Creek when he had lost them both to the wolves.

But then he would have had to tell her the rest of the story, too… of those horrifying days that followed. He wasn't willing to do that just yet. How could he remove the bandages of his tortured soul when the wounds that lay beneath were still raw and unhealed, even after fifteen long years?

The wolves. The damned wolves were always the cause of his painful memories, of his life's suffering. But no matter how many of the beasts he managed to destroy, he knew there were plenty more to take their place. The sheer rage, the burning hatred he held for those timber-dwelling animals could never be quenched. Sometimes he felt like the hatred would grow until it consumed him entirely, leaving nothing but a blackened Stetson and a charred Sharps 50-caliber.

He was throwing more wood on the fire, when the lonesome howling of a wolf pierced the frozen northern wind. Another joined in soon after, as well as a third. It wasn't long before the entire forest was filled with the mournful sound of the pack. It obscured the rush of the approaching blizzard, reaching a frantic crescendo that pressed on Gray's eardrums, threatening to drive him mad even as he stood there. Then it faded, wolf by wolf, until only the moaning of the gale remained.

The hunter shivered in spite of himself, his gloved hands grasping the lean frame of the Winchester until they ached with the effort of holding onto it. He got the campfire blazing bright and hot before retiring to his handmade lean-to, and prayed to God that it would keep the marauders at bay… at least for the duration of the night.

Chapter Fifteen

Timber Gray awoke in the middle of the night, a piercing scream slicing through his slumber like the edge of a well-honed knife. He threw off his blankets and grabbed for his rifle. The blued steel of the Winchester was crusted with ice. As he got to his feet, he realized that he, too, was covered with a light sprinkling of snow which had drifted into the far reaches of his hand-built shelter.

Once again the scream sounded, its frightened tone growing into raw panic. At first, Timber thought that maybe Lenora had been right and the fireside yarns had conjured up some bad nightmares. But the emotion in these screams went much deeper than anything mere sleep could bring.

He ducked out into the night and found himself in the middle of a blizzard. It had arrived an hour so ago, but he had been unaware of it. The hardship of their mountain travel must have unknowingly taken its toll on him, for he had slept through it, his senses lulled into the dangerous sleep of pure exhaustion.

Timber rapped his rifle sharply against the trunk of a tree, knocking ice from the receiver and barrel. He worked the lever and started across the ankle-deep snow of the roadside clearing. The storm raged at a furious pitch. Snow was swirling through the darkness, falling fast and covering the frozen earth swiftly. The blazing campfire was nothing more than a pile of charred ashes now.

The screaming was coming from the dark hull of the wagon and it was the terrified shrieking of a small child. "Miss Sarah," he uttered beneath his frosty breath. As he started forward, he heard an evil snarling accompany the girl's screams. The hungry snaps of a large timber wolf.

Lenora Cook's cries joined those of her daughter and Timber suddenly saw the wolf, its rear haunches protruding over the tailgate of the wagon. The wolfer raised his gun, but the beast lurched backwards out of the buckboard before he could get off a shot. Timber Gray froze for a moment, his heart pounding like a blacksmith's hammer. The wolf hit the snowy ground, dragging Sarah with it. Slavering jaws clamped down firmly on the child's left arm, biting deeply and drawing blood.

Another timber wolf appeared out of the swirling snowfall. It loped toward the struggling pair, its eyes sparkling with bloodlust. Its jaws yawned open, intending to tear into the girl's other arm. An unpleasant memory flashed through Gray's mind then; his boy, Todd, at the mercy of two wolves' hellish game of tug-o-war. But not this time! With a curse on his lips, the hunter leveled the Winchester and stopped the oncoming wolf. A slug caught it squarely in the chest, splitting the plate of its breastbone. The bullet tunneled through the wolf's vitals, tearing through heart and belly, and dropping it in its tracks.

Another shot ended it for the wolf that had hold of Sarah. The rifle cracked. A .44 bullet slammed forcefully into the wolf's temple, spraying brain and splinters of bone into the snow beyond. But, in its death, the wolf's jaws held firm. Timber ran, drawing his Colt as he did. Placing the short barrel of the .45 to the animal's jawbone, he fired twice. The beast's mouth grew slack and Lenora Cook was suddenly there, pulling her daughter's arm free.

Three more wolves sprang from the storm, running from the darkness beyond Timber's lean-to. With the Winchester in one gloved hand and the Colt in the other, he took aim and fired without thinking. Two of the beasts skidded face-down, leaving bloody smears in the fresh snow. The third wolf paid no heed to its fallen brethren. It continued toward the hunter and leaped with a guttural snarl.

Timber lifted his pistol and thumbed back the hammer. The shot caught the wolf in midair, punching through the end of its snout. The slug burrowed into its brain, killing it instantly. The animal spun, head over tail, with the impact, then landed on its back in the snow, no more than six feet from where the wolf hunter stood.

"She's bleeding badly!" said Lenora behind him, but he didn't turn around. There was a commotion going on in a grove of dense firs, where the four mule team was tethered.

Isaiah Cook climbed down from the front of the wagon as Timber walked past, poking the tails of his nightshirt into the top of his britches. "Here," Gray said sternly, tossing the rifle to the young minister. "I'm taking a look in the hollow. If a wolf comes within fifty feet of this wagon, shoot it. Understand me?"

The reverend nodded and took the rifle readily enough. Gray had almost expected a long-winded sermon about the handling of the devil's tool, but Cook remained mercifully silent. Isaiah buttoned his trousers and, Winchester in hand, headed back to where his wife and daughter knelt in the deepening snow.

Timber stopped long enough to pull the Sharps breachloader from its saddle boot and reload the Colt with fresh cartridges. Then he stepped over the iron tongue of the prairie schooner and started off into the trees.

Three of the rawboned mules were to one side of the grove, snorting and cringing in fear, their nostrils flaring with the heavy scent of wolf. The fourth mule was already near death. It twisted and bucked, but its tether held strong, tied to the trunk of a birch tree. Timber sucked in his breath as he ran down into the rocky hollow and saw the predicament the Missouri breed was in.

Wolves covered the animal, seven of them in all. Two clung to the mule's bucking back, while the others darted around and bit at her kicking legs, which were bloody and nearly shred clean of their hide. The mule was a victim of pure hunger, while the little girl, for the most part, had been attached simply for the lust of wanting something to kill.

Timber dropped to one knee and steadied the big buffalo gun. The octagon barrel boomed with the sound of a cannon as the wolfer eased back on the trigger. A wolf fell from the mule's swayed back, most of its head blown asunder. Quickly, Timber opened the smoking breach, inserted a fresh cartridge, and closed the block. The second shot caved in a she-wolf's ribcage, spinning her off into the swirling darkness of the storm.

A wolf with a coat streaked with black turned from its prey and bounded toward the rifleman. Timber had no time to reload. He brought up his .45 and dropped the wolf with a single shot. More of the Colt's rounds kicked up snow near the dying mule. Having had enough for the time being, the other four scurried off into the blackness of the forest, away from the range of Gray's guns.

The bloody mule staggered for a moment, then fell on its side, breathing raggedly. Timber found that he had one round left in his pistol and he used it wisely, putting the animal out of its misery. He then untied the other mules and led them back up the hollow to the wagon.

He tethered them to the seat of the wagon and hurried to the rear. All four of the Cook family were there. Little Sarah cried hysterically while her mother attempted to examine the nasty wound by the light of a lantern. Paul Cook and his father stood there silently, their faces pale. Suddenly, a cold dread filled the hunter and he knelt beside the four-year-old, tossing his Sharps aside and holstering the forty-five.

"Let me take a look at it," he said gently, taking the girl's arm from where it lay cradled in her mother's lap. He lifted the torn cloth of her nightgown from the bloody flesh and examined the wound. It was a nasty one to be sure, reaching from the child's wrist, clean down to her elbow. The lacerations were deep and ragged, but no bones showed and none seemed to be broken. Nevertheless, the wound was bleeding profusely and he knew they had to stop it fast.

"I'll admit, it's a bad one," Timber told them. "But she'll be okay if we can stop the bleeding and get her down to Greybull tonight. There's a doctor there and he should be able to fix her up."

"But how can we stop the bleeding?" asked Lenora. She was still afraid, but had regained most of her composure.

Timber thought for a moment. "Make a sling out of cloth and make it a sturdy one. Then put Sarah's arm in it and pack snow around the wound. The cold should slow the bleeding, at least until we can get to town."

"I understand." Lenora's face was grim as she went to work.

The wolf hunter turned to Isaiah and Paul. "You two come over here with me. We've gotta talk."

The three walked through the blowing snow to Gray's shelter. He knelt down, found his saddlebags, and took a box of ammunition from one pouch.

He placed the box of .44-40's in Isaiah's hand. "Reload and pocket the rest," he instructed. Then Timber thumbed some fresh rounds into the Colt and slung the cartridge belt with the .50 brass over his right shoulder.

"Okay, this is how we're gonna work it," he began, looking the preacher square in the eyes. "I'll saddle a couple of the horses and take your wife and daughter down to Greybull. Shouldn't take us but a couple hours, even in this blizzard. You take those mules and hitch them up to the wagon. There's only three left, but you were a farmer once and should know how to rig up a triangle hitch. I'll be back for you as soon as possible, but I have an idea those wolves will be coming back even sooner. That's why I'm leaving you the rifle. And, mister, you damned well better intend on using it."

Isaiah Cook's eyes were strong and unflinching. "I believe the good Lord will forgive me this one transgression, given the circumstances."

Timber didn't think protecting one's self and the life of his son could be considered much of a sin, but he left it at that. As the reverend went back to the wagon to prepare the team, the wolfer called the boy to his side.

"Paul, do you know how to shoot one of these?" he asked, taking a spare revolver out of the saddlebags.

The boy nodded. "I've been watching you. You just cock the hammer and pull the trigger after you aim, don't you?"

"That's right. Now, I want you to stick that in your belt and I don't want you to draw it unless you absolutely have to. Understand?"

"Yes, sir, Mr. Gray," replied the nine-year-old. He held the six-shooter with a mixture of pride and respect.

Timber dropped a handful of .45 cartridges into the boy's coat pocket. "I doubt if you'll need these, but they're there if you do." In the back of the wolfer's mind, he knew Isaiah Cook might very well lose his nerve or get a crazy notion in his head, and Timber didn't want the boy to be left alone with no way to protect himself.

"You go help your pa with the mules now," he said. "And don't worry none. I'll be back for y'all shortly."

"I'm not afraid," declared the boy bravely. He patted the scarred handle of the Peacemaker. "Not anymore." Then he headed across the snowy clearing to help his father.

Dragging a saddle and blanket in each hand, Timber Gray went to where the horses were picketed. They had been left alone and unharmed during the wolves' nocturnal attack. He saddled and bridled his gelding and, after cutting the supplies off one of the two pack horses, saddled it as well. Before leading them off, he cut the tether of the remaining horse. If the wolves did return that night, at least the animal would have a fair chance at making a run for it.

"Are you ready, Lenora?" he asked, leading the mounts toward the rear of the Conestoga.

"Yes," she replied. She tightened the knot of the snow-laden sling and lifted the child into her arms.

"You can ride, can't you?" Gray asked as an afterthought.

"As well as any man," Lenora told him flatly. There was an expression of cold determination on her face as Timber helped her and the child into the saddle.

Timber Gray climbed onto the black gelding. Rather than returning the Sharps buffalo gun to its boot, he laid it, loaded and ready, across his lap. He didn't much like riding the wolf-infested foothills with only a single-shot rifle, but he knew the Reverend Cook would have better luck with the lever-action than with the .50 breachloader.

Isaiah left his work long enough to walk over to the two horses. He looked up at his wife and, for a brief moment, Lenora saw the man she had married ten years ago. "May the Lord ride with you, my dear," he said softly. Then he turned his eyes to the wolfer. "Take care of them, Timber Gray."

"I surely will," he promised. "I'll be back for you and Paul as soon as I can. And don't forget what I said about using that rifle."

"I won't," said Isaiah. He canted the .44-40 to one lean shoulder. The preacher was without his black hat and the crescent scar stood out on his flushed scalp like the mark of a doomed man. He turned and started back to work on the wagon hitch.

"Let's ride," Timber called over the howling of the wind. "But be careful. We've got a ways to go."

Lenora nodded and pulled her bonnet and winter coat tightly around her. Sarah had ceased her weeping and now sat silently on the saddle in front of her mother, a heavy wool blanket pulled around her shivering form.

Urging their mounts onto the deserted stretch of the old stage road, they lit a shuck through the foothills of the Bighorn Mountains and toward the darkened town of Greybull.

Chapter Sixteen

The town of Greybull started out as nothing more than a lone trading post during the years that men trapped the Yellowstone Valley for furs. The few who dared brave the land of the Arapaho and Shoshone would lash their season's worth of pelts to birchbark canoes and ride the Bighorn River to Abner Halston's trading post. There they could trade their beaver skins for gold, supplies, or strong drink.

Later on, as easterners sought to settle the western frontier, the fur trade bottomed out in the Yellowstone. The wild men who had lived as trappers and hunters finally took brides and settled down. They built up the area around Halston's post and, little by little, formed the town of Greybull. These days, the town prospered mostly from mining and from cattlemen who brought their herds to the Bighorn Valley to graze in the grassy pockets along the western face of the mountain range.

Timber Gray and Lenora Cook reached the settlement an hour after leaving the roadside camp. Their progress had been better than Timber had first expected, mostly because the wind of the blizzard was to their backs and the trail ahead was not yet snowbound. The two late night riders came down out of the foothills, crossed the timber bridge that spanned the icy torrent of the Bighorn River, and trotted their weary horses down Greybull's main street.

The storm had reached a howling crescendo, blowing snow and ice against every clapboard wall and into each shingled crevice. Lenora pulled the frost covered blanket tighter around the shivering body of her daughter as their guide led the way between the double rows of dark buildings.

The first two structures in town were a livery stable and, across from it, a nice two-story house painted as white as the surrounding snowfall. A painted shingle hung over the steps of the front porch, proclaiming J.W. BARRETT — PRACTITIONER OF MEDICINE. Timber and Lenora reined to a halt before the doctor's residence and tied their mounts to a hitching post out front.

As Lenora carried Sarah up the icy path to the front porch, Timber Gray cast a quick glance down the shadowy street. It had been a while since he had last seen Greybull, but then five years had not changed the town very much. Among the businesses along the street were saloons, shops, and even a hotel and gambling house. Trampus Haines' mercantile was still there, having replaced the old trading post years ago.

Gray made it to the house just as Lenora began to knock sharply on the curtained pane of the front door. Soon, they heard footsteps coming down the stairway and saw the faint glow of a lamp inside. The door opened, revealing a dark-haired man in his thirties, clean-shaven and wearing wire-rimmed spectacles. Behind him, holding the lamp, was his wife, a petite woman with honey-blond hair.

"What may I do for you folks?" the man asked, shifting an inquisitive stare from Timber's rugged appearance to the pale frailness of Lenora Cook.

"Are you Doc Barrett?" Timber asked hurriedly. "If so, we've got a hurt girl here that needs your help."

"Please, bring her inside."

They stepped into the foyer, shaking off loose snow and glad to be away from the constant barrage of the winter storm. Doctor Barrett led the way to a small examination room, furnished with glass-paned cabinets and a long, padded table. "Mary Beth, would you start a fire, please?" the young doctor requested of his wife as they passed through a modestly furnished parlor.

"I'll do that, ma'am," volunteered Timber. "You might be needed to help out with the child."

The woman nodded and joined her husband in the adjoining room, closing the oaken door behind her. Timber removed his Stetson, knocked the ice off its brim, and set it on the mantle of the fireplace. He took a few sticks of kindling from the wood box and tossed them into the sooty hearth. After searching the unfamiliar surroundings, he found a box of long stick matches and soon had the fire roaring. Then he settled down into a sturdy, leather-upholstered armchair to wait.

The waiting seemed like an eternity, although it could have only been a short time. Sitting before the warmth of the fire, Timber felt like drifting off to sleep, but he knew that he must stay alert. Lenora and Sarah might be safe in the arms of civilization now, but he knew Isaiah and Paul were still up there in the blizzard. Perhaps the wolves had already returned. If that was so, then that would mean they would have their hands full. With a groan, the wolf hunter left the comfort of his fireside chair and reached for his hat.

It was at that moment that Barrett left the examination room, wiping his hands with a towel. "Sarah is going to be just fine," he told the bearded man. "The wound was deep and she lost some blood, but packing the wound with snow stemmed the bleeding. It was good thinking on your part."

Timber Gray slipped his hat on and retrieved his Sharps from where it leaned beside the front door. "I just figured to stay till I found out that Sarah was okay. Now I've gotta get back up the mountain. There's a couple of folks still up there and close to thirty wolves."

"Wolves," echoed the doctor, recalling the nasty gouges of Sarah's wound. "Then you'll need some help. Give me half an hour and I'll round up some men to go with you."

"Ain't got the time to waste, Doc," Timber told him flatly. "I've gotta ride now. But I'll tell you what you can do. Just tell old Trampus Haines over at the general store that Timber Gray is riding for trouble on the old stage road. He'll move like a scalded hog in getting up a posse."

"I'll tell him," promised J.W. Barrett, pulling a heavy coat over his flannel nightshirt.

"Jefferson," called Lenora from the door of the examination room. "Bring Paul back to me safely… and Isaiah, too."

"I'll surely do my best," he told her, then ducked back into the swirling snow. He and the doctor parted company at the street, Timber untying his black horse and climbing into the saddle, while Barrett headed down the sheltered walkways toward Haines' store.

"Let's go, boy," he said and spurred the gelding back up the frozen trail for the foothills. With one hand holding the reins and one resting on the stock of the buffalo gun, he rode. The familiar clinch of fear built steadily in the pit of his gut. He feared for the lives of Isaiah and Paul. He also feared that the blinding drift of the snow and the savage wind could very well throw his shot off a few fatal inches, and end up getting someone killed for the mistake.

But, strangely enough, the only thing Timber Gray didn't fear were the wolves themselves. The only emotion he reserved for the marauding pack was one of pure hatred. A hate, he swore, that would burn like wildfire until he had purged the western wilderness of every last wolf he could set his sights on.

Chapter Seventeen

Timber heard the gunshots as he neared the trailside camp. They echoed in quick succession, but the high pitch of the howling wind and the mad sweep of the blizzard distorted the reports, making them seem distant and muffled.

The black gelding knew where they were headed and, sensing its rider's urgency, moved forward in a gallop. Timber let it take the lead, for the snow was coming down so thick that he could scarcely see a yard ahead of him. The horse made good time, surefooted and confident, despite the scent of wolf that permeated the air.

Timber strained his numbed ears, but could hear only the deafening rush of the storm. The shots had ended. The hunter's sheepskin coat was bundled tightly about him, but the sharpness of the wind penetrated the heavy clothing and chilled him clear to the bone. Ice began to form on the graying bristles of his beard, while his hat brim sagged with the weight of accumulated snow.

For a moment, as he rode along the frozen trail, Timber thought he heard a low growl from up ahead. The wind continued to whistle and whip around his ears and he dismissed the sound as nothing more than the storm. But he didn't take any chances. He cocked back the big hammer of his Sharps as the gelding neared the grove of firs and the clearing it enclosed.

"Isaiah!" he yelled against the roar of the wind. "Isaiah... where the hell are you?"

No one answered. He reined his horse off the trail and suddenly heard the snarling again, this time sounding like more than a trick of the wind. A dark mass hurled itself out of the blizzard. The horse reared with a frightened cry, then writhed in sudden silence as the timber wolf bit deeply into the animal's gullet. With a curse, Timber lifted his rifle. But as the wolf's fangs ripped through muscle and arteries, the agony grew too much for the gelding. It bucked wildly, eyes wide and glazed with panic. The hunter felt himself falling backward, spinning out of the saddle.

He landed hard on his back, the impact knocking the breath from his lungs. He sat up, aware that his hands were empty. The Sharps had fallen from his grasp and he had no earthly idea where it was.

"You'd best get a hold of yourself, Timber," he told himself as he staggered to his feet. "If you don't, you're gonna die out here in these woods for sure."

Timber's horse stumbled a few yards away, the wolf's death hold draining the animal of its strength. The horse collapsed with a heavy thud. Dark blood gushed from its mortal wound, staining the newly-fallen snow an ugly crimson. Timber slipped the thong from his Colt and laid his hand on the butt. He was about to draw and fire his weapon, when a savage growl sounded directly behind him.

The hunter began to turn, but the wolf was already upon him. The weight of the beast hit him squarely in the back, knocking him sprawling into the snow. He felt the wolf's claws dig into the material of his coat, ripping, searching for his flesh. The warm wetness of slaver splashed down Timber's bearded cheek as the wolf's teeth gnashed dangerously close to his neck. With a shudder of revulsion, he reached back, caught a fistful of fur, and yanked the animal completely over his head. It landed heavily on its back, its eyes burning like coals, its fangs snapping and straining for the softness of human flesh and the coppery taste of blood.

Before the wolf could get to its feet, however, Timber reached beneath the folds of his coat and drew the bone-handled knife from its sheath. With a wolfish grin of his own, he raised the knife and plunged its slender blade into the animal, just below the brisket. He twisted the knife downward, slicing and hacking through the wolf's innards with a viciousness born of pure contempt. After the last twitch of life left the wolf, he withdrew the skinner and returned it to his belt.

Timber got to his feet. He walked a few faltering steps and saw where his horse—the magnificent black gelding with three white stockings—laid cold stone dead in a snowdrift. Two wolves tore at the horse's body, bloodlust flashing in their eyes.

He felt for his pistol and found it still in the holster. "You just killed a damn fine horse for nothing, you filthy devils!" he gritted. He put a .45 slug through the right eye of one and another through the temple of the other.

Spotting the Sharps lying a few feet away, he retrieved it and brushed the loose snow from its receiver. In the swirling paleness of the snowstorm, he caught quick glimpses of low forms darting from tree to tree, encircling the clearing like an advancing army. Timber knew they had to get out of that forest and fast. He saw the dark hull of the wagon with its milling team of nervous mules and started toward it.

Where is Cook? he wondered, beginning to think that perhaps the preacher had high-tailed it into the woods, leaving the boy to fend for himself. "Isaiah... where in Sam Hill are you?"

He moved on through the deepening drifts and abruptly stumbled over the partially covered carcass of a dead wolf. He cast his eyes over the frozen ground and saw three more wolves lying dead in the snow. Then he spotted another body and his heart sank in anger and despair. Isaiah Cook laid there, his darkly cassocked body sprawled near the wagon's front wheels. The wolves had done him in swiftly, dragging him down by the legs and then tearing into the tender flesh of his belly and throat.

The young minister had not died in the dishonor Timber Gray had expected of him, however. Cook had died bravely, the Winchester held firmly in his stiffening hands. The four wolves nearby were testament to his courageous stand.

"I'm sorry, preacherman," whispered Timber, gently prying the rifle from the man's blue fingers. "So damned sorry."

Abruptly, the boy came to mind. Where was Paul? Surely he was still alive, for Gray had heard shots only a few minutes before and they had been from a .45 pistol and not from Isaiah's rifle. The wolfer trudged around the rear of the covered wagon to where the canvas covering was drawn securely over the lip of the tailgate.

A single wolf lay near the rear wheels. A flap of canvas still hung between its clenched jaws. A bullet hole glistened above the animal's left eye where Paul had shot it with Timber's revolver. Without hesitation, Timber pulled himself onto the tailgate and stuck his head through the laced canvas opening.

He was greeted by cold darkness and the crisp click of a gun's hammer being cocked. "Hold on, partner," he told the boy. "It's just me."

Paul Cook's frightened breathing sounded from the far corner of the wagon bed and he sobbed in relief. "Mr. Gray! You're back!"

Timber Gray climbed further into the wagon and laid his rifles aside. Paul tumbled forward and they met in a clutching embrace. Timber could feel the dampness of the boy's tears through his shirtfront and he felt relief at having gotten there in time... for the boy's sake, if not for his father's.

"Are you all right, son?" he asked, looking the frightened boy in the face.

"Yes... but Pa... Pa's dead!" he cried. "He shot four of those wolves, but this big one came out of nowhere. A big white wolf with a limp."

Timber knew the animal well. "Cripplefoot!" He spat the name out as if it was some foul cussword.

The wolfer wanted to say something more to Paul, something to console the youngster and ease the grief he must be feeling, but he knew there was no time. "We'd best get going whilst we can, Paul. What about the mules? Have the wolves gotten to them yet?"

"They tried, but I ran them off." Paul held up his pistol. "Even shot down a couple of them."

"Good for you," said Timber. Together they crawled over the Cooks' jumbled possessions and reached the front of the wagon. Timber cocked both his rifles and leaned them against the wagon seat. Then he and Paul took their places and gathered up the ice-encrusted reins of the mule team.

"What about Pa?" asked Paul as Timber whipped the reins and drove the team out onto the old stage road.

"We're gonna have to leave him for now, son. But don't worry. I promise to come back for him. I swear he'll have himself a decent, Christian burial."

The hunter's promise calmed the boy. Timber turned his attention back on the swirling darkness that stretched ahead of them. Black forest reared on both sides of the trail, thinning as they descended the foothills toward the open expanse of the Bighorn Valley. It was slow going as they made their way down to Greybull, but the team moved at a sure and steady pace. Isaiah Cook had done a fine job with the triangle harness, distributing the burden of the wagon equally among all three mules.

Then, as they reached a sharp bend in the trail, Timber saw half a dozen forms dart into their path. As the team and its wagon reached the turn, the wolves ran along side, biting and snapping at the hooves of the Missouri stock. One wolf leaped in and nipped the lead mule's ankle, drawing blood and pain, before a flashing hoof nearly decapitated the pesky beast. The dead wolf rolled off into the darkness, while his five brethren continued to run the team into a frightened frenzy.

Timber handed Paul the reins. "Here. Keep them in the middle of the trail if possible. I'm gonna do me some sharpshooting."

The wolfer took his Sharps and cocked back the hammer. Lifting the big gun to his shoulder, he picked his first mark. With a thunderous report, the 50-caliber let loose with its single load. A large wolf at the left collapsed, its spine blown in half by the heavy grain bullet. Timber still wore the cartridge belt over one shoulder. He plucked a fresh round from it and quickly reloaded. A second shot from the buffalo gun took another wolf's head clean off. The downed animal tumbled beneath the mule team and was trampled into the churning snow beneath their hooves.

Three more to go. Timber got them with the Winchester, levering rounds into the breach as fast as he could fire them. One by one, the animals fell to well-placed .44 slugs. Every hit was a fatal one and the hunter knew there would be three more hides to skin out when he made it back into foothills. Or *if* he made it back, Timber thought grimly.

Onward they drove, down the curving trail to the snow-blanketed valley below. Once, Timber glanced back past the side of the wagon and saw wolves following them. He couldn't say for sure, but it looked like the remaining number of the pack. Rather than try to risk his balance and shoot at them, he decided to outrun them, or at least attempt to. Greybull was not far away. He could see the fork of the two rivers ahead as the wagon charged down a steep grade toward town.

"We're gonna make it, Paul," Timber called over the howl of the storm. Then he turned his eyes back on the snowy trail and grabbed for the rifle once again. Something was moving out in the darkness ahead of them. More wolves? If they were, Timber swore he was ready for them. He levered a round into the repeater's breach and rested his finger tentatively on the trigger.

But as they neared the approaching forms, he recognized them as riders. The townspeople of Greybull were coming to their aid. There were a dozen men in all, armed with rifles and scatterguns. Barbers, storekeepers, and businessmen powered their mounts forward, passing the wagon and heading after the now retreating pack. Timber heard an arsenal of guns go off and he even saw one oldtimer ride past with a Colt Navy pistol in each hand.

A lone rider pulled up along side the slowing wagon and Timber saw that it was his old friend, Trampus Haines. "We'll run these critters back into the hills, Timber," he yelled. "You get on into town, but use some caution. The bridge is all iced over and it's mighty slippery!"

"Much obliged, Trampus," returned the wolfer as he took the reins from the boy and drove the mules past. He threw one last glance back and saw Haines galloping off after the others, a long-barreled Peacemaker in one hand.

A few minutes passed. Then the trees thinned and he saw the sturdy timber bridge that spanned the river. On the far side, stood the dark buildings of Greybull. Slowing the team, he intended on driving the wagon across carefully. Trampus had been right. There was a glassy coating of sheer ice on the planks of the bridge floor. And that was enough to unnerve any man, especially with the cold depths of the Bighorn River coursing swiftly underneath.

But as they started across the bridge, only a few yards from safety, Timber Gray heard a throaty growl in his ear. He jerked his head around to see the lean countenance of a white wolf staring at them from the opening in the canvas directly behind them. It was Old Cripplefoot! He had been in the wagon since they had left the roadside clearing. The wolf's eyes seemed to sparkle with triumph as his fangs snapped out and snagged the lobe of Timber's right ear.

"Dammit!" growled the hunter, pulling back the reins before remembering exactly where they were. The mules attempted to stop, but their shod hooves did nothing but slip and slide on the icy boards of the bridge. The lead mule fell and was trampled by the others of the team. Abruptly, the wagon turned sideways, angling toward a railing of the bridge. If they went through and over the side, they would be lost.

Timber forgot about Cripplefoot and grabbed Paul by the arm, holding the barrel of his Sharps in the other hand. "We've gotta jump, Paul. Right now!"

The posse of Greybull's citizens were returning down the trail, when they saw the covered wagon crash through the side railing and plunge into the frigid depths, dragging the last two mules with it. "Lord Almighty!" proclaimed Trampus, and they all rode down to the bridge together.

When they got there, they sat on their horses and stared silently over the side at the rushing water. No sign of wagon or mule team could be seen. "Done swept a mile or so downriver, I'd say," voiced the oldtimer gravely. "And you said Timber Gray was driving that there wagon, did you, Trampus?"

Haines removed his hat, as did the others. His lean, mustachioed face bowed in sadness and he nodded. "Yes, he was. And not a finer wolfer ever there was in the whole blamed territory! He'll be sorely missed, old Timber Gray!"

Then, out of the darkness, came a voice like that of a ghost. "Save your eulogies, Trampus. The only thing I'm ailing of is a busted knee and it ain't serious enough to go burying me over."

The riders turned their startled eyes down the length of the shadowy bridge to where Timber Gray stood, bruised and battered, using his Sharps for a makeshift crutch. Paul Cook stood beside him, cradling a broken arm, but very much alive.

"Well skin me and nail my hide to the smokehouse door!" said Trampus. "I surely thought you'd done yourself in this time, Timber."

"Quit your jawing and give me a hand," said the wolf hunter. "The boy here has a busted arm. We need to get him over to Doc Barrett's as soon as we can."

"We'll see he gets there," said a robust man Timber recognized as Sheriff Henry King. The lawman lifted the boy into the saddle and rode across into town. The others followed, leaving Timber and Trampus standing on the bridge alone.

"What's eating at you, Timber?" asked Haines as the bearded man stood at the broken railing, staring solemnly down into the dark, churning waters.

"Trampus… it was Old Cripplefoot," he told the storekeeper. "He was there, right in the wagon with us." Timber reached up to the side of his head and his fingertips came away wet with blood. "The mangy critter took off a piece of my ear, too."

"Well, then I reckon he went down in the river with the whole kit and caboodle," said Trampus. "Got what was coming to him, I'd say."

Timber Gray lifted his eyes and, slowly, a grim smile crossed his lips. "Afraid not. Take a look over yonder."

Trampus followed his friend's gaze to the far bank of the river. There, on a timbered ridge, stood a lone wolf as white as the snow itself. For a long moment it merely stared at the two men. Then it let out a triumphant howl that surpassed the fury of the winter wind. A gust of snow blew across the river and, when it cleared, Old Cripplefoot was gone.

"The Ghost Wolf," muttered Trampus, his voice soft with wonder.

And, for one brief moment, Timber Gray was almost willing to agree.

Chapter Eighteen

Three days after the blizzard had blown further southward, Timber Gray felt the urge to ride again. He had grown bored of sitting around the potbelly stove in Haines' Mercantile with nothing better to do than play an occasional game of checkers and swap old stories with some of the locals. There had been some talk about bounty hunters riding hellbent through the Bighorns; Elijah Cox and his boys it was said. It was also said that Jess Ramsey was with them. Timber hadn't known who the boy with the fancy gun was during their encounter in Burial Pass, but he did now. Ramsey had a reputation as a gunfighter with a quick draw and a sure aim. Folks said the boy from Alabama had gunned down a dozen men during the past couple of years and the wolf hunter knew that he would try his hand at him, if they ever crossed paths again.

Timber's knee was badly bruised, but nothing had been broken and he was bound and determined to not allow it to slow him down. The first day the clouds cleared and the sun peeked over the broken range of the Bighorn Mountains, he knew that it was time. Buying a couple of good pack mules and a spirited, gray roan from the livery stable, Timber outfitted himself with a new Winchester, ammunition, and a few days worth of supplies.

He did not ride alone. Trampus Haines, who was an old friend from his buffalo hunting days, saddled himself a horse and took his worn Henry repeater from the rack over the door. As he tugged on his hat and headed for the door, Haines' dour-faced wife protested his leaving.

"You took something mighty precious from me when we married, woman," Trampus told her sharply. "And, despite your infernal nagging, I intend to have it back, if only a few days!"

Myrtle Belle Haines gave him a scolding look, but did not press the matter any further. Trampus had been a better husband than most and she knew, deep down, that he deserved his time in the mountain air.

The storm had dumped several feet of heavy snow on the wooded slopes of the foothills and even more on the higher peaks. It took some doing, but the two men made it up the old stage trail in a day's time. As they traveled the abandoned road, they discovered the frozen carcasses of eight wolves half-buried in the snow. On up the trail they found the lone pack horse that Timber had cut free several nights before. The animal lay dead in a snowdrift, the eighteen wolf pelts still lashed securely to its back. It had frozen to death in the midst of the snowstorm, unable to find sufficient shelter even in the dense trees that grew so abundantly on the mountain's western face.

They reached the clearing by nightfall. The following morning, Timber searched the area near the pine grove. After he and Trampus had picked through the heavy drifts, fourteen more wolves were uncovered. Timber thought back to that frantic night and realized just how very lucky they had been. It was nothing short of a miracle that they had made it out of the foothills alive.

The bodies of the twenty-two wolves were frozen solid, so the two men gathered wood and built a roaring fire. One at a time, the wolves were hung over the flames until they thawed enough to be skinned. That night, over hot coffee and beans, Timber Gray totaled his kills since leaving the Whittaker ranch. Forty wolves had fallen to the wolfer's guns. That meant there were still ten left up there in the Bighorns, including the most valued prize of all… Old Cripplefoot.

Before leaving the next day, they readied Isaiah Cook and lashed his blanketed body to a mule's back with rawhide and rope. They had found the young preacher where Timber had left him that fatal night. His dark cassock was stained with blood, his eyes glazed over with frost, and his pale hands forever clutched a Winchester rifle that was no longer there.

"I didn't much cotton to all his ravings about hellfire and damnation," Timber told Trampus. "But if the good Lord gives merit to bravery, then this man's last hour surely bought him a mansion in heaven."

The storekeeper nodded respectfully. "You ready to ride?" he asked from the back of his spotted sorrel. There was a flush of new vitality in the man's face, a sparkle in his eyes that had not been there days before. The ride into the mountains had done old Trampus a world of good, thought Gray.

"I reckon so." But as the two riders started leisurely back down the trail for Greybull, Timber turned in his saddle and stared off toward the rocky face of the mountain range. A sound had whistled in his ears for a brief instant. Perhaps it had only been a cold mountain breeze moaning through naked trees or the call of a snow hawk on a distant peak. But he could not help thinking that it was the howling of a wolf, beckoning to him from the lofty wilderness above the timberline.

"Soon," he promised beneath his breath. His gray eyes lingered a moment longer, then turned back to the winding trail ahead. Yes, soon he would return and the confrontation would take place. The final confrontation between the hunter and the hunted.

A day or so later, Timber Gray was sitting in a rocking chair, smoking a hand-rolled cigarette and staring idly through the icy panes of Haines' store window. The iron stove was toasty warm and the store smelled of tanned leather, spices, and kerosene. Trampus stood behind the long oaken counter taking inventory on a recent shipment of canned goods, while Myrtle Belle was busy with her sewing in the back room. Timber could hear the steady cranking of her new-fangled, foot-pedaled sewing machine as she worked on a blue calico dress.

Directly across the street from the mercantile stood the Central Overland Stage office. That morning, a flurry of activity was going on outside. A bright red Concord coach with gold trim stood before the office entrance. Men loaded the coach's front and rear boots with baggage and mail, while Able Jones from the livery harnessed a six horse team into place.

"Hey, Trampus," called Timber, tossing his smoke to the floorboards and grinding it underfoot. "I didn't know the Overland was heading out this morning."

"Yep," said Haines. He parked his stub of pencil behind one reddened ear and joined his friend at the window. "The stage road going up to Crystal Falls is clear now and they've got a week's worth of mail to deliver. Heard they're taking some passengers with them, too. Lenora Cook and her young'uns."

Timber Gray was surprised by the news. "I wasn't told about their leaving," he said, trying hard to hide the disappointment in his voice.

Trampus shrugged. "Maybe she thought it best to leave quietly. You might not have noticed, old friend, but that lady has taken quite a shine to you. So have the children."

The wolf hunter said nothing. Secretly, he felt the same way they did. Since leaving Tennessee, every child he had come across had brought nothing but bitter memories of the son he once had. But Paul and Sarah had vanquished those harsh emotions and raised his paternal instincts once again. Since coming to Greybull, they had looked to him as a substitute father of sorts. And Lenora... well, there was something much stronger between he and Lenora, even though neither of them had found the courage to make their feelings known as of yet.

"I'm going for a walk," Timber said. He took his coat and hat from a hook by the door and slipped them on.

"All right," replied Trampus, returning to his work. "You be sure and tell Mrs. Cook and her little ones goodbye for me."

"I'll do that," agreed Timber. He closed the door behind him and stepped off the boarded walkway into the dirty snow of the street.

Jones and the other men greeted him as he walked past. He threw up his hand in return, then strolled down the walkway to the stage office's double doors. He saw Lenora and the children sitting in the spacious waiting room as he came in, all decked out in their best traveling clothes. Their baggage, with their few remaining possessions, sat at their feet.

"Mr. Gray!" yelled the two youngsters as they ran to him. He put an arm around each and walked them back to the bench. Their mother sat there quietly, her face pale and her eyes regretful.

"I had no idea you were leaving today, Lenora," Timber said. He tried to generate a smile, but failed dismally.

The woman stood, her frail hands fidgeting nervously with her handbag. "I was going to tell you, Jefferson... I swear I was. But I knew it would be so hard. For the children... and for me."

"But where will you go?"

Lenora Cook smiled timidly. "Perhaps we'll go back to Minnesota or settle somewhere in these parts. I hear there's work for a widow like myself in Miles City. The stage clerk suggests we stay at the Demorest Hotel there... until I make a decision."

"But..." Timber started, then caught himself. He knew what he had been about to say. That those youngsters shouldn't grow up without a father and a woman like Lenora shouldn't try to make it without the support of a good man. But who was he to say such things? He was nothing more than a drifter; a scraggly hunter of wolves who had lived in the wilds most of his life. No, he had no right to say such things or have such thoughts for a proper lady like Lenora Cook.

He reached in the pocket of his sheepskin coat and took out a roll of banknotes. He peeled off a few crumpled bills. "Ma'am, I believe I owe you some money."

Lenora was puzzled. "How do you figure that?"

"Well, your husband and little Paul here, they shot a few of those wolves I skinned a few days back. I figure I owe you for about six or seven of the hides at least."

The woman pushed the greenbacks aside. "I'll not take money from you, Jefferson Gray. If anything I should be paying you. You saved me and my children from dying out there in that godforsaken wilderness and, for that, you'll have my gratitude and respect forever."

Timber reddened in embarrassment and stuffed the paper money back into his pocket. "To me, that's worth its weight in gold," he told her. Then he frowned grimly. "But I couldn't save Isaiah. That's what gores me most of all."

A shadow fell across Lenora's face at the mention of her late husband. "Isaiah... the man I married... was lost years ago, Jefferson. He died the day that mule kicked him in the head."

The stage clerk peered from the barred window of his ticket booth and motioned to them. "Mrs. Cook, the stage is all ready to go."

Timber picked up their carpetbags and they all went outside together. After the parcels had been secured to the coach, the hunter stooped and looked at both children. Sarah held her china doll tightly, while Paul stood there with his broken arm in a sling and his head held high despite his sorrow.

"Now, you take good care of your ma, you hear?" Timber told them quietly. "She's gonna need all the help she can muster and you two are just the ones who can give it to her."

"We will, I promise," declared Paul. He and his little sister both had tears in their eyes as they climbed into the belly of the stagecoach.

Timber took Lenora's thin hand and helped her up. He held it a second longer than he intended to and found himself staring into soulful eyes. They stared at one another for a long moment, then Lenora spoke. "You deserve a better life than the one you're leading now, Jefferson," she told him. "And that life could be yours... simply for the asking."

Timber Gray opened his mouth and, out of all the right things he could have uttered, he could only manage to come out with the wrong one. "Have a safe trip," he said. He released her hand and she took her seat between her son and daughter.

Reluctantly, Timber closed the coach door and stepped back upon the dirty boardwalk in front of the Overland office. The driver cracked his whip and the horse drawn coach surged westward out of town. It would travel the stage road to Crystal Falls, then onward to Myer's Junction and finally to Miles City.

The wolf hunter stood there for a long time, feeling more alone than he had in years. He thought back to Lenora's parting words. Had she really been offering him the chance of a better life? Surely he had misunderstood her intentions. No decent, God-fearing woman would be willing to put up with a no-account wolfer like himself.

He was in a dark mood as he crossed the slushy street to Haines' store and, right away, he knew the only remedy for such a feeling. He had to get back up to the mountain, back to the tracking and hunting that he had been hired to do.

Timber Gray walked straight to the counter of the mercantile, not bothering to even remove his hat and coat. "Trampus, I need you to fix me up. I'll need coffee, beans, salt pork… a couple of weeks worth. And I'll need more ammunition. .45's and .44-40's."

Trampus Haines looked at his friend over the top of his spectacles. "You going back up the mountain already?"

"I have wolves to hunt."

The storekeeper removed his glasses and poked them in his vest pocket. "Then I'll be going with you."

"Afraid not, Trampus," Timber told him flatly. "It started out as just another hunt, but it's turned kind of personal now. What with Old Cripplefoot and all."

"Seems to me it's always been personal with you and those varmints, even before the Ghost Wolf. What is it between the two of you? I know you lost your family to the critters back in Tennessee, but seems there's more to it than that. Ain't it about time you told somebody about this grudge of yours and what's really behind it?"

Timber avoided looking at his friend. "There is something I never told you about what happened that day on Chestnut Creek. You see, I was bitten by that wolf that I killed. And that wolf was… rabid."

"Lordy Mercy!" said Trampus. "But I've heard tell there's no cure for someone who's been bitten by a diseased critter."

"I'd heard the same, too. And, at first, it seemed that it was so. No more than a few days after I'd buried Rebecca and Todd, I began feeling almighty sick and dizzy in the head. Soon the illness became worse. I could eat nothing and the thought of drinking water sent me into a panic. It wasn't long before the madness set in. I began seeing things that weren't there. I'd wake up in the middle of the night, bathed in a fevered sweat, and see my wife and son standing at the foot of the bed. They'd just stand there and stare at me, their clothes ripped and bloody, and their throats torn out. As the disease worsened and the images grew more horrifying, my mind snapped completely. I set the cabin afire and ran off into the woods, wild-eyed and crazy.

"I don't rightly recall much about those days of madness. Folks told me afterwards that they could hear me in the dead of night, screaming my lungs out up on the highest peak of the Smokies. I even staggered into town once, mumbling insanely and sputtering foam like the head on a beer. I had me a big ol' tree limb in hand and folks locked their doors, afraid that I might do them harm. A couple of the best sharpshooters in those parts even considered putting me out of my misery, but nary a one could bear to do so, being good friends of mine and all.

"I surely would have died of that godawful sickness, if I'd not come upon an old Cherokee medicine man who had stayed on in the mountains after his people had been forced to walk the Trail of Tears. I was beyond knowing anything then. I collapsed at the edge of his camp and he took care of me. He tied me to a sourgum tree for my own good. Then he brewed some sort of concoction made out of berries and roots, and poured it down my gullet, though my belly could scarcely

122

endure it. It was a month after I'd first been bitten that I awoke, weak and shaky, but thinking clearly. It wasn't long before that Indian had me up and healthy once again. But there was one thing he couldn't cure me of and that was my hatred of wolves. The very name of the beast sent me into a rage and still does. The only thing that seems to keep me from returning to that awful madness is the destruction of the creatures. And so I've spent the past fifteen years with my gun primed and loaded, itching to put a bullet into any wolf that chanced to cross my path."

After he had finished his painful story, Trampus could only stand there and shake his head. "I do declare! I never knew it went that deep, my friend. I figured we all thought you to be a little touched in the head, hating wolves that much. But I can see your reasons now." He turned and began to gather the supplies Timber had requested. "But if you go riding for Cripplefoot, you'd best take care. That critter is bad medicine. You could find his teeth in you before it's over with."

Timber chuckled. "He already got the ear," he said, pointing to the missing lobe. "He'll not get a chance to claim another piece of me without one hell of a fight."

Trampus Haines grinned beneath the shaggy droop of his mustache and began to pack the vittles in brown butcher paper. If a wager on Old Cripplefoot's fate had been made, he would have bet a twenty dollar gold piece right then and there. For if any man alive could lay to rest the legend of the Ghost Wolf, it was the man who stood across the counter from him.

Chapter Nineteen

Solitude.

Every man, no matter how reserved or rambunctious, needs a little every now and then. Some men find it in books, some in hard work, others at an empty table in the dark corner of some smoky, cowtown saloon. For Timber Gray solitude meant riding where few men cared to roam. He felt that lonesome peace as he made his way through the wooded foothills east of Greybull and back into the mountains from which he had come. But this time the cleansing isolation came less easily than usual. Spending a week in town had changed him, spoiled him for human companionship and the sound of a friendly voice. Every time Timber passed a familiar bend in the trail, he found himself thinking of his journey with the Cook family and that, in turn, reminded him of Lenora and the children.

With two fresh pack mules and the slate gray roan, he ascended the slopes of the Bighorn, his eyes searching for the first sign of wolf tracks. The thick stands of pine, cedar, and fir thinned as the hills gave way to the mountain range. The stony peaks reared above him and the trail was lined with snowy boulders and the gnarled stumps of weathered trees. The great pinnacle of Cloud Peak loomed a few miles in the distance. Although he couldn't say for sure, Timber had a strong feeling that Cripplefoot and the remaining members of his pack were up there somewhere, holed up in one of the many canyons or gorges.

He found day-old tracks as he prepared to make camp for the night. They encircled the meatless bones of a hamstrung deer; their last kill before heading further westward. Putting beans and coffee on to boil, Timber constructed a shelter between two leaning boulders and picketed his animals nearby. One of the pack mules toted the wolfer's provisions, while the other awaited the burden of future hides. The pelts that Gray had previously claimed were now locked in the storeroom of Haines' market until he got back with the final ten.

The following day, Timber Gray started for Cloud Peak. He took Willow Pass into the high country, aware that heavy drifts from the blizzard might make the way impassable at times. But, fortunately, he had no trouble getting to where he was going. Morning drew on into afternoon, followed by evening and the cooling of nightfall. The tracks of the ten were still clear to see. Gray knew he would have to make better time if he was to catch the pack before they reached the tail-end of the Bighorns and vanished across the open plains of the Powder River Valley.

The hunter found them early the next day. He had left the close confines of the pass, traveling along the snowy rim of the canyon. The wind was strong and frigid there, and no trees grew on the rim to cut the sharpness of the mountain breeze. Timber Gray was considering going back down into the pass, when he heard the sound of wolves ahead. Further he rode, until he stood upon the rocky lip of a box canyon. Securing the horses at a distance, Timber took his saddlebags and rifles and crawled along the rim. He found a clear spot just above the canyon floor where he would be well hidden from the pack below. Only a sheer drop of two hundred feet separated the hunter from his prey, so he had no trouble seeing what they were up to.

Ten wolves occupied the canyon. Some worked off a recent meal of elk, while the older wolves, Cripplefoot included, lounged beneath a twisted willow tree. Two males were busy running a long-eared jackrabbit, more out of mischief than hunger.

Timber crouched on the ridge for a long moment, watching the pack below. To someone who knew nothing of wolves, their actions would have seemed peacefully innocent at that moment. But Gray knew the beasts better than he knew most men. Wolves were like the rest of God's creatures in many ways. They raised families and lived to a ripe old age, active in the hunt until the pack weeded the feeble from the fold. But they had a dark stain on their souls; the hunger, the savage bloodlust of a devil. In the progressive expansion of the West, wolves were considered more than killers. They were regarded as a natural catastrophe, like storm or flood. Many a cow had fallen to the fury of the animal, as well as a few good men. It was when the wolves' appetite and wanton need to kill reached such extremes that cattlemen and townspeople hired hunters and trackers... men like Timber Gray.

Taking his time, the wolfer checked his Winchester, then the big Sharps. Both guns were fully loaded and ready to do their job. He settled himself at the lip of the canyon, then took the buffalo gun and sighted down the heavy octagon barrel, searching for his first target of the day.

He knew the initial shot would be the crucial one. It always was where large numbers were concerned. The exit of the box canyon was only fifty feet from the nearest wolf and, when

Gray pulled that gun's trigger, they would be out of his range and down the pass in only a matter of seconds.

Timber knew his most promising mark would be the wolf nearest Willow Pass, but he just couldn't resist the temptation that lay, apparently unconcerned, beneath the denuded limbs of the twisted willow tree. With a tight grin on his bearded face, Timber settled his iron sights on Old Cripplefoot, aiming at the white wolf's skull, right between the eyes.

He was on the verge of squeezing the trigger, when Cripplefoot's ears perked in sudden alertness. The wolf lunged from his spot in the snow just as the 50-caliber slug drilled a large hole in the trunk of the tree. As the shot echoed through the canyon like the report of a cannon, the others of the pack followed their leader, heading for the pass that continued further up the rocky mound of Cloud Peak.

"How the hell did he know?" Timber cursed, tossing the Sharps aside and grabbing up the repeater. Standing atop the rim, he brought the Winchester to his shoulder and levered the first cartridge into the breach. Cripplefoot was already gone, as well as a few others. He picked off a wolf as it reached the mouth of the pass, hitting it directly behind the left ear.

Two more wolves fell to .44 slugs. The impact sent them rolling, one hitting the hard wall of the canyon with bone-shattering force. Four more wolves lunged for the pass entrance, almost at once. Timber fired again. A bullet hit a male in the thick fur of its neck, shattering the vertebrae and dropping it instantly. They were all through but one now and it only had a few feet to go. Timber fired just as he reached the crevice. The rifle's lead barely missed its mark, skimming across the wolf's hindquarters, drawing blood, but not fatally.

Timber Gray stood quietly on the snowy ridge, letting the last of the gunshots fade in his ears. The entire barrage had taken less than ten seconds and, yet, he was exhausted. Grimly, he totaled his kills. Four wolves lay sprawled on the trampled snow of the canyon floor. Not as many as he had hoped for, but it still whittled the pack's number down by a considerable few.

He untied his animals and descended into the box canyon. After eating a brief meal of salt pork and hardtack, he busied himself with the wolves at hand. It took him an hour to skin out the four and lash their hides to the mule. After that, he returned to the fire, poured himself one last cup of coffee, and thought about Old Cripplefoot and the surviving five. He knew where they were going. They would be heading further up the pass to a spot called Wolf Gorge. The gorge was actually a small valley nestled midway on the elevation of Cloud Peak. There was water there, all year round, as well as plenty of game. Many a wolf had sought refuge in the gorge, as well as men running from the law.

Few knew how to reach the mountain haven. Having traveled the Bighorns before, the wolfer not only knew the location of the gorge, but had discovered an unknown shortcut that would get him there hours ahead of the pack. All thoughts of Greybull and the Cooks driven from his mind, Timber Gray prepared his outfit for travel. In his mind, he was already beginning to concoct a fool-proof trap for Cripplefoot and his five followers. A trap that would require a little ingenuity, as well as a little luck.

Evening was falling upon the mountain when the bearded hunter reached Wolf Gorge. The entrance to the secret canyon was well hidden and anyone unaware of its location would have passed it by, unsuspecting, and continued on up the trail. Two jagged boulders leaned toward each other, making a natural entrance just high enough to accommodate a horse and its rider. The crevice was concealed with thick brush and scraggly evergreens. The heavy powdering of snow furthered the illusion of a solid canyon wall.

The sky was awash with soft colors as the sun set far to the west. The gray roan was apprehensive at first as his rider urged him toward the thick growth, but he moved forward as he discovered a clear opening beyond the thicket and smelled the promising scent of clear mountain water. The mules followed passively. One carried the canvas pack of supplies, while the other toted the four wolf pelts and a bighorn sheep. Timber had shot the ram back down the trail a piece, intending to use it as bait for his trap.

Once inside the hidden gorge, Timber sat in the saddle and studied the canyon. It was scarcely five hundred yards across on all sides, its walls craggy and steep, except for the one directly opposite the entrance. There, above a thick grove of pine and spruce, was a rocky shelf and the dark opening of a small cave. A clear stream of pure mountain water cascaded down the rocks of one wall; ice melted from the lofty slope of Cloud Peak itself. It collected in a large basin near the pine grove. Timber led his animals there to be watered.

As the wolfer picketed them near the basin edge, he remembered the last time he had stayed there in the gorge. It had been the spring of '76 and he had tracked a lone grizzly there, one that had killed a couple of Harve Patterson's finest breeding studs down in the settlement of Bingham. It had been breathtakingly beautiful then, the trees budding with new shoots and the canyon floor lush with spring grass and a rainbow of fragrant wildflowers. His springtime thoughts did nothing more than make him feel the winter chill even more, so he pulled his fleeced collar tighter against the wind and tramped through the snow to his mules.

He went to work immediately, cutting the ram from the swayed back of a mule and dragging it to the center of the canyon. There, he tied the sheep's two hind legs together and, pitching the rope over the limb of a gnarled oak, hefted the carcass off the ground. He tightly secured the rope, letting the ram hang there, its curved horns barely touching the frozen earth. His bait set, Timber did his best to cover his tracks and went back to conceal his horses.

He led the three animals into the shadowy depths of the pine grove. He unburdened them and tied them where the mountain breeze could not spread their scent and alarm the approaching wolves. Timber took his rifles and saddlebags, then started to the far wall of the canyon, where the cave was located. His plan was to hole up in the cave and await the pack's arrival. Then, as they tugged and tore at the fresh meat of the dall, he would pick them off one by one. Timber had used the tactic several times before and had always been successful with it.

The hunter was about to leave the pine forest, when he spotted something in the snow at his feet. There had been a light dusting the night before and a thin coating of virgin frost layered over the old snow of last week's blizzard. Digging the heel of his boot into the snow, he uncovered a splattering of frozen blood.

The discovery gave Timber cause to worry. Shifting his rifle to a more comfortable position, he started forward. Suddenly, he spotted something lying near the boulders at the base of the canyon wall. He found it to be a horse. It was a sturdy buckskin mare with an old Denver cow saddle strapped to its back. The animal was dead, having taken an ugly dose of double-ought buckshot in the left side, just above the saddle's stirrup. But the wound had not killed the horse immediately. No, it was plain to see that the buckskin had been fired upon somewhere outside the secret pocket of Wolf Gorge and its rider had managed to get her to shelter before it collapsed of blood loss.

Looking down at that nasty wound in the horse's ribs, Timber thought of the sawed-off shotgun he had seen hanging from Elijah Cox's saddle a week or so ago. The bounty hunter's ten-gauge would have produced such a devastating wound and Timber was betting that it had. That meant the horse had been carrying someone the bountymen were gunning for. And Timber had a pretty good idea who that man was.

The hunter spotted a speckled trail of blood on the snow that had settled in the cracks of the boulders, leading up to the hole in the wall. As he climbed the rocks and neared the cave entrance, Timber slung his saddlebags and Sharps over one shoulder, and cocked his Winchester. Not knowing exactly what to expect, he fisted his gloved hands around the stock of the repeater and stepped into cold darkness.

Chapter Twenty

When it came to unexplored caves, Timber Gray seemed to draw nothing but bad luck. On dozens of occasions, he had found himself walking into the black depths of some mountainside crevice. Sometimes he found them damp and empty, except for a few bleached bones or fragments of broken pottery; the legacy of a long forgotten occupant. But the majority of his cavernous ventures produced some type of unexpected danger. He had encountered all manner of creature, from hibernating grizzlies to mountain lions to renegade Indians. Once, when crossing the Ozark Mountains back in northern Arkansas, Timber had bedded down and awakened the next morning to find himself surrounded by a family of razorback hogs… and they hadn't exactly been in a neighborly mood.

The cave on the craggy wall of Wolf Gorge was a different story however. He had made the small cavern his home several times in the past, while on hunts or just passing through. The extent of the cave was etched in the wolfer's mind like a permanent map, one that he referred to now as he moved further into the dusty darkness. It was seven feet from granite floor to ceiling, maybe eight or nine in width. The length of the cave was sixty feet and it crooked into an elbow bend at one point. There the cave gave way to a small chamber where a man could stretch out and build a fire without fear of the flames or smoke being seen from the outside.

Although few knew of it, there was an opening further down the passageway, barely large enough for a good-sized man to squeeze through. Beyond that, on the far side of the gorge, was a hidden pass that led straight down the mountainside to Barren Creek. Many an outlaw had used the escape route to dodge lawmen that were getting too close for comfort.

With his finger resting lightly on the trigger of his rifle, Timber Gray moved further into the cavern, pausing only to let his eyes grow accustomed to the pitch darkness. As he neared the bend in the passageway, he caught the bitter scent of woodsmoke from a fire that had been quickly smothered. Timber turned the corner with the barrel of the repeater directed ahead of him. He squinted against the inky blackness, his eyes barely making out the dim red glow of warm embers on the cavern floor. A small, almost undetectable sound echoed from the far side of the smoldering fire. Without hesitation, Timber shifted his Winchester toward a shadowy form.

"Who's there?" he demanded.

Silence. Then, after a long moment, the voice of a man answered. "I have a pistol here. Aimed right at you."

"And I've got a Winchester on you," informed the wolfer calmly. "So why don't you just start that fire back up, before one of us gets hurt."

Timber Gray listened to the man's ragged breathing as he thought over his visitor's suggestion. Finally, there was motion and a flame from a sulfur match brought the gray ashes and loose wood blazing back to life.

The two men looked each other over thoroughly in the flickering glow. Each was suspicious, their weapons held steadily upon one another. As curious eyes studied Gray's rugged form, the hunter also took time to size up his adversary.

The man was a Negro in his late twenties, lean in build and muscle. He wore the timeworn clothing of a cowboy; flannel work shirt, cowhide vest, woolen britches, and muddy, thorn-scarred boots. The left leg of the man's trousers was saturated with dried blood. A dirty red bandana was bound securely around the fellow's wound, just above the knee. He wore a gunbelt of tanned leather, from which the man's Remington revolver had been drawn.

Timber recognized the face immediately and recalled where he had seen it last. A roughly sketched portrait on a crumpled wanted poster.

"You're Luke Bell, ain't you?"

The cowboy's eyes were as steady and cold as the pistol in his hand. "What're you? Another bounty hunter?"

Timber shook his head. "I'm a hunter, but not of men. Wolves are my game, as well as bear and cougar when they get to troubling folks."

They stared at one another in silence for a long moment. The nervous edge had eased a bit, but still their guns remained cocked and aimed. Timber's eyes once again settled on the man's wounded leg. From the amount of blood lost, he figured Bell had been hit with buckshot rather than a single bullet.

"Did Elijah Cox do that to you?" he asked.

"So that's who he was," replied the cowhand in sudden realization. "Knew he was bounty hunter, but didn't know his name. I reckon he and those others have been tracking me for the better part of a month now, from Colorado all the way up here to Wyoming."

"They say you killed a man."

Luke Bell spat in disgust. "That's a damned lie if there ever was one. Just because I played a few hands of poker with the gent and had some hard words with him afterwards, they done gone and pinned his murder on me. Well, it ain't true! Not one blasted word of it! I'd tell Elijah Cox that, too, if he'd stop shooting at me long enough to listen."

"I don't think Cox is the least bit interested in whether you're innocent or guilty, Bell," Timber told him. "It's that thousand dollar price on your head that's got him all riled up."

The black man nodded. "That and the chance for an old-fashioned lynching, maybe?"

Timber agreed. "You may be right about that."

Luke lifted his Remington and settled its sights on the wolfer's shirtfront. "You sure you ain't figuring to claim that bounty for yourself?"

"Like I told you before, my hunting's limited to wild critters, not outlaws. The name's Timber Gray and all I want to do is share this here cave for a while. Then I'll be on my way."

The fugitive returned his pistol to its holster. "I know of you, Mr. Gray. In fact, I was hired on at the Triple Bar Ranch near Santa Fe when you bagged that cougar back in '74. Biggest cat I'd ever laid eyes on."

"And one of the meanest," added Timber, canting the Winchester to one shoulder. "Got a mess of scars across my ribs to prove it, too."

Luke grinned at the recollection. "Yeah, you rode onto the ranch with that big wildcat bound to the back of a mule. No bullet in him, just a knife wound from belly to brisket, as pretty as you please."

The wolfer was flattered at the cowboy's remembrance, even though the kill hadn't been quite as clean as Bell thought. A vicious swipe of the lion's paw had sliced him up badly and knocked the gun plumb out of his hands. He nearly had to gut the big cat with his hunting knife before it finally gave up the ghost.

Timber leaned his rifle against the cave wall and crouched beside the warm fire. "How long have you been holed up in here, Luke?"

"A couple of days maybe. But I don't know how much longer I can take it. Ain't had a bite to eat since yesterday morning and this wound is surely paining me something awful."

"Well, I'll tell you what," proposed the hunter. "Why don't I go round up some supplies and fix us some supper. I'll put on some beans and a pot of coffee and you can tell me your story."

The wanted man nodded in appreciation. "Sounds like a fair deal to me."

Half an hour later, night had fallen. The fragrance of beans and bacon and strong black coffee filled the cavern, the rough granite walls flickering orange with the glow of the fire. Timber handed the cowboy a tin plate heaped with food. Luke wolfed it down hungrily and then started on seconds.

After the skillet had been emptied and their mugs were refilled, Luke opened up and told his tale. "I grew up on a plantation down south in Georgia. I started out life as a slave, along with my folks. Pap and Mammy were field hands, working the cotton and tobacco. I was just a child then, but worked in the stables and the barnyard mostly. By the time Mr. Lincoln's Proclamation came about, I'd become quite a hand with both horses and livestock. I was fourteen years old when I took advantage of my newfound freedom and rode down to Texas to find work. It was tough going at first. Most white folks were still sore about losing the war and they were reluctant to hire on a black man. But I soon proved myself and was hired by one of the biggest outfits in the southwest. A few years with Charlie Goodnight made me into a top hand where cattle drives were concerned and I started hiring out to other spreads. Stuart, Whittaker, Shanghi Pierce... I've worked for them all at one time or another. Drew top pay, too, despite the color of my skin. That's because I can rope, brand, and ride as good as any sagebrush veteran and shoot the head off a blowfly at twenty paces.

"I'd just finished with a trail drive down in New Mexico last fall and it was nearing winter, so I headed for Colorado, hoping to grubline until spring round-up. I stayed on with a few folks, doing odd jobs for a meal and a place to bunk. But it wasn't long till I got cabin fever and headed for town. I had me a nice stake and was aiming to get my fill of whiskey and winnings before heading on to Montana."

"So you rode into Durango," replied Timber. He set his battered cup aside and fished his tobacco pouch from his shirt pocket.

"Yes, sir, and it proved to be my downfall." Luke Bell's voice was heavy with bitter regret. "After having me a couple of shots of Red-Eye, I found a poker game going on in a joint called the Golden Nugget. Only three other players sat at that table besides myself; Dan Spencer, who was the town mayor, a snaggle-toothed Mexican, and a cattleman from Denver. We played a civil game for a while, until I spotted Spencer's bottom deal. I spoke up and told him as much. He was halfway drunk by then and cussed me up one side and down the other. Said I was sore because I lost and threatened to draw on me if I didn't scat outta there. Now, I just might've chanced a gunfight right then and there. I'd heard he was a downright poor shot with a pistol, especially when liquored up. But there was the fact that he was a white man and that most of his friends in the saloon were white, too. Lucky for me, I wasn't drunk enough to take his challenge. If I had and won, I'd found myself dangling from a length of hemp in a matter of minutes. So I skedaddled out of the Nugget and rode north the next day."

"What happened then?"

"Well, I got to Cripple Creek and met up with a fella I'd herded steer with down in El Paso. He showed me that blasted wanted poster and said I was being sought for the murder of that cheating mayor. Seems that Spencer was found dead in an alley the morning after I'd left, his lapel sporting a new buttonhole and his gold stolen. Since we'd had harsh words over that poker game, the Durango sheriff figured me as the best suspect. So now, every lawman and bounty hunter in the territory is out to get my black hide."

Luke looked across the fire to see Timber Gray staring at him, his face expressionless, his thoughts hard to read. "I didn't kill that man, Timber. I've shot me a few rattlers in my time, but I ain't never fired on a man in anger."

Timber believed the young cowpoke. Since coming west, the wolfer had grown to know the men who drove cattle for a living. Some were prone to drinking and some were gun happy, but the majority were hard working, honest men. In Timber's opinion, they were the most trustworthy breed that a man could deal with. He had banked on many a cattleman's word and, as he shared his fire and grub with the wounded fugitive, he began to trust Luke Bell and consider him a kindred spirit of sorts.

"I reckon I got spooked after leaving Colorado," Luke continued. "I rode north, hoping to make the Dakotas before Christmas. But then Cox and his white trash buddies started hounding my tracks and I took to the Bighorns. I thought I'd shaken them when I was heading up the pass for the gorge here.

Cox hit me in the leg with that confounded scattergun of his. Hit my horse, too, but didn't even know it till old Buck collapsed down near the pines."

They sat there in silence for a long while. The tale had been told and now each man turned it over in his mind. "What're you gonna do, Luke?" Timber finally asked. "Just keep on running till someone puts a bullet through your brain-pan and throws you across their saddle?"

"Hell no!" declared Luke. His eyes were bright and sharp against the contrast of his ebony face. "I'll not have it end that way. Lord knows I've thought it over enough, Timber, and it seems the best thing would be to go on and turn myself in. I'd surely be facing a hanging, but I'm willing to take that chance. The running, the hiding like a frightened animal... I lived like that once, under the whip and scared of the overseer's shadow. Now, with Cox and his men, I feel like that frightened little slave boy again. And I can't bear the thought of spending my last hours on this earth bound by those chains again."

As their conversation drifted back into thoughtful silence, Timber Gray found himself comparing Bell's plight to that of another fugitive, one that had roamed the mountains for years, dodging well-placed bullets and angry posses. Old Cripplefoot had been wanted for nearly forty years now, by both the Indian and the white man. But one thing set Luke and Cripplefoot apart. The Ghost Wolf deserved the label of renegade, for his victims had been many along the trail, as well as those of the wolves that followed him. But this hardworking cowboy who sat across the fire from him was the total opposite. Timber had known few black men during his life, but this one seemed as true and honest as any white man he had come across in his travels... maybe even more so. And he deserved a chance to clear his name from the crime he was accused of and continue his life... as a free man.

"Are you certain about giving yourself up?" he asked the cowboy.

Luke Bell said that he was.

"Then I think the best thing to do is to ride down the mountain to Greybull. There's a sheriff there by the name of Henry King. He's a good lawman and a fair one, to boot. Never heard him say a wrong word about nary a man, black or white. If anyone can clear up this mess and give you a fair shake, it's him. I'm willing to ride down with you, if you'd like."

Luke shook his head. "I can't ask you to do that. It's my trouble, not yours. Besides, you've got those wolves to track."

"That pack can wait," Timber assured him. "You're bad hurt and need a doctor's care. You'll get that in Greybull, too."

"But Elijah Cox and his men," protested the cowhand. "They're still gunning for me, hoping to bring me back drilled and dried. You'll be caught in the crossfire."

Timber Gray would not be discouraged, though. "Don't worry about me none. This old hunter can handle himself, be it a gunfight or a barroom brawl. Anyway, a couple of those fellas swore to kill me when we met up in Burial Pass. I figure we're bound to butt heads sooner or later, and I'd just as soon get it over with."

"All right then," said Luke Bell, declaring defeat at his new friend's stubbornness. "We'll leave at sunrise."

After a while, each man bedded down beside the fire and began to drift to sleep. Before slumber crept up on him, however, Timber Gray lay there and stared up at the cavern ceiling. He thought of the men they might happen upon during their treacherous descent down Cloud Peak. He wasn't very worried about the Delaney Brothers or the hot-headed kid with the ivory-handled Colt. He had handled their kind before and he could do it again, if need be.

But the others—Elijah Cox and Avery Gimble—they were ones to be reckoned with. Timber had encountered their kind during the War Between the States; Missouri farmboys who had chosen to follow violent leaders such as Quantrill and Bloody Bill Anderson. They were guerilla fighters, men proficient with horses and guns. The wolfer found himself thinking of Cox's sawed-off shotgun and his brace of .44 Dragoons. Such weapons were deadly in the hands of a man who could use them and Timber was sure the bounty hunter could, and would, use them to the best of his ability if they crossed their path during the long journey down to Greybull.

Chapter Twenty-One

The sound of gunfire echoed over the canyon wall, sending Timber Gray scrambling for his rifle and up a stony ridge lined with snow and dead brush.

That morning, before dawn, he had taken his horse and the two mules out of Wolf Gorge, packing Luke Bell's cow saddle along as an afterthought. He went back down the pass a few hundred yards to a fork in the trail. Taking the route to his right, Timber rode further until the pass petered out into little more than a goat trail. Any other man would have turned back right then and there. But the wolfer, like a few others, knew where the pathway actually led. Soon it widened once again and flared into a broad trail bordered by high canyons and steep snow-covered slopes. He was in the hidden passageway that led from the rear of the gorge cave, all the way down Cloud Peak to the Bighorn Valley below.

Timber had picketed the animals near the narrow cave exit, transferring the wolf hides to the supply mule and saddling up the other for Luke. He was tightening the cinch under the mule's belly, when the crack of rifle reports ricocheted out of the gorge and caught his attention.

Cocking the Winchester as he made his way to the top of the canyon wall, he crouched low and moved carefully to the lip. Concealed behind the flat face of a boulder, Timber peered down into the gorge at the cause of the ruckus. Elijah Cox and his fellow bountymen had somehow found their way into the hidden canyon. How their discovery had come about was unimportant. All that mattered now was that they were there in the flesh and armed to the teeth.

"Might as well come on outta that hole, Bell," yelled the band's leader. "You stay in there much longer and you'll die anyhow, if not from our bullets, then from cold and starvation. Might as well come on out in the open and face the music." For emphasis, Elijah unholstered one of his .44 Dragoons and unleashed a barrage of thunderous shots.

The sudden spurts of gunsmoke singled out the bounty hunter's position at the edge of the piney woods. The other four were scattered nearby, hiding in the shelter of evergreens and outcroppings of rock. Timber could hear the men's horses somewhere on the far side of the grove. He knew if he could get them in sight, he just might be able to buy him and Luke some time. Not.much, but perhaps enough to get a head start down the hidden pass and off the mountain before nightfall.

Timber heard the rolling report of the big .50 Sharps explode from the mouth of the cave below him and was glad that he decided to leave it with the cowhand for safekeeping. Luke's aim was much better than he would have expected, for it sent splinters flying from a tree only inches from where Cox was hiding.

"I'm innocent, I tell you!" growled Luke from back inside the cave. "So why don't you just let me be?"

143

"Ain't nothing personal," chuckled Avery Gimble from the center of the grove. "Our line of work calls for chasing down yellow-bellied varmints like yourself, innocent or guilty. Whether you come back to Colorado riding in a saddle or slung over one, don't make no never mind to us."

The bounty hunters waited for a reply, but received nothing but silence. "Well, what about it, Bell?" snarled Cox, his snaggletoothed leer as ugly as sin. "Ain't you got an answer for us?"

"Yeah," said the Negro, sending another .50 slug booming into the thicket of pines. "Ya'll can go straight to hell!"

Elijah Cox unsheathed his other pistol. "Lay it on him hard and heavy, boys," he said with a grin. "This one ain't gonna come easy."

The five fired as one, sending a volley of shots at the entrance of the cave. Rifle and pistol slugs and the spreading swarm of buckshot rained toward the entrance. Some projectiles struck the canyon wall, sending slivers of rock and shale into the crisp morning air.

While the Cox gang was busy whooping it up and wasting ammunition, Timber Gray was making his way along the canyon rim with the patience of a seasoned hunter. His attention was not centered on the men in the grove, but the five horses tethered beyond, near the freshwater pool. As he edged along the northern wall of Wolf Gorge, Timber spotted the animals and the trees they were tied to. He reached the cover of a leaning boulder. Taking careful aim from a kneeling position, he found his mark and fired. The first slug from the Winchester missed, but the following shots did the trick. The rawhide tethers parted cleanly under the hunter's expert marksmanship. Soon, the five mounts were freed from their restraints. In a fit of panic, they galloped southward through the gorge and toward the opening.

"The horses!" yelled one of the Delaney brothers, immediately forgetting Luke Bell and the reward he would bring. "Someone shot the horses loose!"

All gunfire ceased and Timber could see Cox and his men leaping through the pine forest, hellbent for their horses. The thought of being stranded on Cloud Peak with no horses or provisions was a sobering one to the bountymen. Fortunately for the wolfer, it was precisely the reaction he had hoped for. As they followed their mounts out of Wolf Gorge and down the narrow pass beyond, Timber knew that he and Luke must make good use of the reprieve and get a move on. He climbed back down into the hidden passageway and found Luke standing there, leaning near the rear exit. He held the Sharps canted to one lean shoulder and favored his buckshot leg.

"Pretty fancy piece of shooting you did," said Bell with a grin of admiration. "Takes a mighty steady aim and a good eye to snip a rawhide thong at that distance."

Timber slid the repeater back into its boot. He swung into the saddle of his roan and motioned toward the other mount. "Hope you don't mind riding that old mule there. Might be rough at first, but it'll be a steady ride down."

Luke pulled himself into the saddle, the once effortless action now hindered by his injured leg. "Timber, I'd ride a banty rooster down this confounded mountainside if it would get me away from the likes of Elijah Cox and his bunch." He leaned forward and started to hand the big Sharps and its ammo belt back to the bearded hunter.

"Hang onto it," Gray advised. "I've got me a feeling we might meet up with trouble. You may have need of it before we reach the bottom."

Luke Bell didn't question the man's instincts. He merely inserted a fresh round into the Sharps, closed the breach, and followed the wolfer down the pass. Whether he was riding toward salvation or damnation, Luke had no idea. But with Timber Gray as a guide, he felt he at least had a fighting chance. If trouble was to cast its dark shadow on their path, Timber knew it would happen at Mountain Cross. The Cross was located on the western face of the Bighorns where the rocky canyons began to gradually give way to sloping foothills. It was a strange configuration of trails where two passes crossed each other's path.

Three things set heavily on Timber's mind, each one an obstacle that could prevent the two from making it to the valley safely. First, there was snow. It clung haphazardly to the four sloping points of the Cross. Like Burial Pass, a loud shout or a single gunshot could send snow sliding down in a crushing avalanche. There was even the chance that a slide had already occurred and they would ride into a blockade of snow and ice, cutting off their route of escape.

Secondly, there was Elijah Cox and his men. Shooting the horses loose had merely been a diversion. They would have caught up to their fleeing mounts by now, hot under the collar and itching to use their guns. The bounty hunters might have stumbled upon Wolf Gorge purely by accident, but then someone in the gang could be familiar with the Bighorns. They might possibly know of the hidden pass Timber and Luke now traveled and be riding down the adjoining trail to head them off. The Cross was not a place to face your enemies down, especially when there were five of them and only two of you.

The third—and most remote—danger that might confront them would be the wolves. Timber Gray knew the beasts far too well to exclude them from the picture. Wolves had an unnerving way of showing up in the most unlikely spots and, since Old Cripplefoot and his dwindling pack had yet to reach Wolf Gorge, Timber figured them to still be somewhere on the mountain. He could not afford to rule out the possibility of coming upon them in one of the many canyons that led up the face of Cloud Peak.

They rode at an even, unhurried pace all morning. The floor of the pass was covered with hardened snow and, even though the horse and mules were surefooted and born of the mountain breed, they took it easy. There was the risk of a thrown shoe or a twisted ankle to keep in mind and, in the situation they were now in, such injuries would prove fatal, for both the animals and their riders.

Dark, boiling clouds had rolled in during the night. They covered the vast Wyoming sky and hid the rays of the winter sun. The clouds hung ominously with the threat of snow and Timber knew there would be a few inches of fresh powder on the peak before tomorrow morning. It was afternoon now and he had no opportunity to worry about the hardships that nature might bring. They were fast approaching Mountain Cross and, although Timber wanted to ignore the feeling, he sensed that they would meet up with disaster there.

After another hour of riding, they reined their horses to a halt. "Is that the Cross up ahead?" Luke asked him.

Timber nodded quietly. He looked over at Luke and wondered if the cowboy was going to make it. The long hours of riding had aggravated the gunshot wound, causing it to bleed again. Several times he had nearly toppled from the saddle in sheer exhaustion. "How are you holding up?" he asked the black man.

"Never mind me, Timber," Luke told him flatly. "It's the Cross we'd better concern ourselves with. Once we get past it, we'll be home free."

The hunter knew he was right. He turned his eyes suspiciously toward the junction of the two passes that flared into a small basin at the center. All in all, it looked too much like a tidy trap to Timber Gray. But there was no turning back now. All they could do was proceed and pray to God that his haunting suspicions were dead wrong.

"Keep close and be ready," said Timber. He slid his rifle from the boot and laid it across his lap. "But don't fire unless you have to. If I'm gonna be buried, I want it to be permanent and not just until spring thaw."

Their rifles at the ready and their senses alert, the two moved forward down the pass toward the middle of Mountain Cross. They could only see clearly into the pass opposite them; the one that led westward to the valley and the town of Greybull. The other one, which headed from north to south, was obscured from view until a rider came directly upon them.

Timber urged his roan onward. His ears were primed for the least little sound, the faintest echo that could forewarn them of intruders ahead. A lonesome mountain breeze moaned mournfully against bare stone and snow, making the task even harder. Suddenly, his horse snorted nervously as it caught the familiar scent of other horses nearby. By the time Timber heard the quiet blowing of other animals, it was too late. They had already ridden into the junction of the Cross and stopped in its center.

The wolf hunter and the injured cowpoke glanced sharply to their left.

There, in the southern entrance of the adjacent pass, sat five overcoated riders. Elijah Cox grinned triumphantly on the center horse, while Avery Gimble, Jess Ramsey, and the Delaneys stood to either side.

"Well, look a here now," said Cox. "If it ain't our old friend, Timber Gray. Should've known it was you who shot our horses loose back in that gorge. Only a dead-eye shot could've pulled such a stunt."

Timber began to lift his Winchester, intending to end it right then and there. But the bounty hunters had beaten him to the draw. Their guns were already leveled at the two riders. "You bring that rifle up another inch, Gray, and I'll blow you clean outta that saddle," said Elijah. The muzzles of his ten-gauge never wavered from the wolfer's chest.

Luke Bell spoke up, hoping to appeal to the bountymen. "All right, so you caught us. It's me you want, though, not Timber. Let him be and I'll give myself up to you."

Elijah scratched the bristles of his chin thoughtfully. "Naw, we can't let ol' Timber Gray get off that easy. He put down me and my chosen profession once and I ain't one for forgetting." The bounty hunter regarded the bearded man coldly. "You got any more smart-alec comments about me and the boys, you just have at it, wolfer. It's likely to be the last words you utter."

Timber stared at the ugly black pits of the shotgun's double bores, then shifted his attention to Elijah's golden grin and dangerous eyes. The hunter swallowed his intended words, for he knew if he spoke his mind, Cox would surely lose his temper and fire.

"Let me have the old man, Elijah," the kid asked his boss eagerly. Jess Ramsey sneered venomously at the wolf hunter. "You told me I could if we ever crossed paths again."

"I reckon I did at that," agreed Elijah. "You've been itching to put lead to a body since we left Cripple Creek. Anyway, we got what we came for, so I guess you're entitled to a little fun."

"Much obliged," said Jess. Timber watched as the kid smoothly drew his ivory-handled Colt from its studded holster. The cold light of the winter afternoon reflected on the silver gun, highlighting each cut and scroll of the fancy engraving. It would have almost been an object of beauty, if not for the deadliness of its contents.

"Are you really gonna take the chance of bringing all this snow and rock down on us?" Timber asked the boy, casting his eyes to the sloping walls of the Cross.

Jess snickered. "You really expect me to fall for that trick again? You must be stupid or mighty desperate, old man."

Gray looked toward the group's leader. Elijah Cox just shook his head. "I'm with the kid this time. Seems like a mighty feeble play for someone with a reputation like yours, Gray."

The bearded hunter swept his eyes across the gang, raking each ugly face with his steely gaze. "Then you're all just a bunch of natural-born fools."

Elijah's silly grin faded and he spat forcefully into the snow. "Shoot him, Jess, before I shoot him myself."

Ramsey cocked the hammer of his .45 and centered the sights on Timber's belly, the spot that would bring the most agony before death. The wolf hunter thought about bringing his own gun up, but knew Jess would have him plugged three times before he could even unleash one round from the Winchester. He glanced at Luke Bell almost apologetically, then braced himself for the shock of lead tearing through his innards.

But Jess never found the chance to pull the trigger. Timber Gray watched as the kid's expression changed from pure hatefulness to a sudden bewilderment and, yes, even fear. The wolfer was puzzled at first, then realized that the kid's attention was no longer focused on him. Ramsey's eyes stared past the hunter, as did the eyes of the other bountymen.

"Good God Almighty!' exclaimed Luke Bell somewhere behind him.

Timber took the chance of ignoring the boy's gun and turned toward their point of interest.

There, in the pass directly opposite of the one Cox and his men occupied, came Old Cripplefoot and five large timber wolves. They gave their enemy no time to think. Abruptly, they lunged through the center of the crossed passes and were upon the horses before anyone had a chance to react. Timber was surprised when the wolves ran past him and Luke, directing their furious attack solely on Cox and his gang. However, the shock was not potent enough to keep Gray from taking advantage of the sudden turn of events.

"Quick... down the pass!" he yelled to Luke. Both men spurred their mounts forward, trying to put as much distance between them and the others before the inevitable happened.

And it did, a moment later. As the wolves leaped and snarled, and the bounty hunters' horses bucked wildly, trying to avoid flashing fangs, Cox and his boys emerged from the confusion, brandishing their guns. That was their mistake. A barrage of misplaced gunfire echoed throughout the adjoining passes, sending a tremor through the very heart of Mountain Cross. The crack and boom was suddenly overshadowed by a much more thunderous and frightening roar. It was the deafening sound of snow and rock sliding off the faces of the slopes, into the veins of the crossed trails.

Timber Gray glanced back only once before urging his slate gray roan faster down the pass toward the foothills. All he could see was a massive torrent of snow and ice sliding downward, filling the spot where they had stood only a few seconds before. The wolves and the bounty hunters were obscured from view and Timber had no idea whether they had been buried in the slide or had escaped it as they had.

"Looks like we've left our worries behind us, Timber!" yelped Luke Bell, his rawboned mule keeping pace with the hunter's roan.

Timber wasn't so sure, though. Half of him wanted to believe that it was the end of it all. But the other half—the cynical mistrust of the loner—still had its doubts. Foes like Cripplefoot or Elijah Cox and his men were not adversaries to

151

be taken lightly. Timber would not be at all surprised if both wolves and bounty hunters had survived the avalanche at Mountain Cross. And, if that turned out to be the case, then both would be coming after him with a vengeance.

Chapter Twenty-Two

"You've brought me more patients in the last few days than I've had all winter long," J.W. Barrett told Timber Gray as they helped the injured cowhand up the snowy walkway to the doctor's front porch.

"Never meant to by choice, Doc," admitted the wolfer. "I just seem to run across these wounded critters on the trail every so often."

Luke Bell chuckled weakly and fought against his dizziness, holding onto the Sharps rifle for support. "Very funny, Timber. Now why don't you just keep your jokes to yourself and get me inside before I pass plumb out."

The doctor's wife held the door open as they carried the Negro inside the two story house. Soon, the three had made it to the examination room. Luke lay on the padded table, while Doc Barrett took a scalpel from a metal tray and began to cut away the matted fabric of the man's bloodstained trousers.

Barrett grimaced at the wound just above Luke's left knee and began probing. After a long moment of careful examination, the physician called to his wife. "I'll need clean towels and a basin of hot water."

"Am I gonna lose it, Doc?"

J.W. Barrett looked into the haggard face of the fugitive and smiled. "It's a nasty wound, but no bones were hit and there's no sign of blood poisoning. You'll walk again, but with a limp most likely."

Luke swallowed dryly and laid his head back on the table. He closed his eyes in total exhaustion and grew silent.

"You're in good hands now, Luke," Timber told him. "If you don't mind, I'll tend to the horses and then head down to the general store for a while."

"You go ahead, Timber," said the cowhand. "And I'd just like to say... well, I'm mighty obliged to you for getting me down off that mountain."

"Rest up," Gray told him. "I'll be back directly and we'll talk about what we discussed back in Wolf Gorge."

Doctor Barrett accompanied the wolf hunter to the door and studied him as he slipped his dirty silverbelly hat over his graying head. "What in tarnation is going on here, Timber?" he asked. "That man's got a load of buckshot in his leg and, from the spread of the pellets, I'd say from a sawed-off shotgun."

"I won't lie to you, Doc. It was bounty hunters. Luke Bell is wanted for the murder of Dan Spencer of Durango. He claims to be innocent of that crime and I believe him."

The doctor removed his eyeglasses and absently cleaned them with a handkerchief. "Fixing up the fellow's leg is one thing, Timber, but I'll let you know up front, I won't harbor a fugitive from the law."

"And I don't expect you to, Doc. When I get back, me and Luke are going to talk to Sheriff King. Luke is tired of running. He wants to turn himself in and take his chances at getting a fair shake."

Barrett nodded solemnly. "All right, I'll agree to that. Just wanted to let you know where I stood."

Timber Gray walked down the snowy path to the hitching rail at the edge of the doctor's yard. He took the gray roan and the two mules and started across the street to the livery stable.

The clouds that now hung over the mountains had dumped a light snow on Greybull the previous night. A fresh blanket topped the roofs of the town's buildings and clung to the eaves of the covered walkways. It was now nearing evening and the town's single street was already deeply rutted with the tracks of many a shod horse and buckboard wagon.

Able Jones pushed the double doors of the livery open as Gray came up.

After exchanging greetings, the wolfer stabled the animals. He unsaddled them, rubbed them down, then saw that they received their share of oats and water. Timber left his supplies lying on top of a stall fence and gathered up the wolf pelts, tying them together at the tails.

"See you only got four of them rascals, Timber," said Able. He sat at the far end of the livery, his feet propped before the warmth of a potbelly stove and his eyes glued to the pages of a dog-eared dime novel. "What became of the others?"

"Got away… for now," Gray replied.

"Forty-four wolves is danged good for one hunt," the man told him. "Nobody would blame you if you wanted to leave it at that."

"Nobody but myself." Timber Gray took his Winchester from its boot, slung the wolf hides over his shoulder, and headed out the door.

He was heading down the boarded walkway to Haines Mercantile, when he came to the Cattleman Saloon. Glancing through the panes of the big window, he saw that the place was uncrowded and that the long mahogany bar was deserted except for the bartender. "A stiff shot of whiskey would go down good right about now," he told himself and stepped inside.

The establishment was inviting, both in surroundings and in the warmth of the big iron woodstove in the corner. All the tables were empty, except for one where a poker game was taking place. The players looked up curiously as the wolfer closed the door behind him, then returned their eyes to the cards that had been dealt to them.

"Howdy, Timber," greeted Sonny Dill, setting aside the beer mug he had been polishing. "Just come down from the mountain?"

"Yep," said Gray. He laid the wolf pelts at the brass foot rail and removed his deerskin gloves, stuffing them into his coat pocket. "Bring me a bottle of rye and a glass. I need to burn this chill outta these old bones."

"Coming right up," said Sonny, turning to fetch the man's request.

Timber had taken his first shot and was turning to glance out the front window, when his heart skipped a beat. There, riding across the timber bridge into town, were four very familiar horsemen. It looked as though Elijah Cox and his boys had escaped the crushing weight of the avalanche, or at least most of them. The Delaney brothers seemed to have caught the brunt of the snow slide. One of them lay across a saddle, wrapped in a woolen blanket, ready for the undertaker. The other was more fortunate. He had only suffered a broken arm and a few minor bruises.

The wolf hunter leaned against the bar and watched as they rode slowly into Greybull. Avery Gimble and the wounded Delaney stopped at Doc Barrett's place and Timber knew there would be some trouble there. Luke still had the Sharps buffalo gun and his Remington pistol, but was he in any shape to use them against seasoned killers? Elijah Cox rode on down the street to Haines' store, while Jess Ramsey made a beeline straight for the Cattleman Saloon.

Timber Gray turned back to his bottle and downed another shot of liquor. "Maybe you'd best get down to the other end of the bar, Sonny. I'm expecting some trouble."

The barkeep looked out the window and saw the kid swinging down off his horse. "Good luck to you then," he said and ambled down to the far end of the counter, away from the line of fire.

The wolfer laid his .45 on the bar and placed his left boot on the brass foot rail. He trained his eyes on the mirror behind the bar and watched the saloon door with grim expectation. The shuffling of cards had come to a halt. The men who had once been interested only in winnings were now attentive to the event that would take place within the next few minutes.

Timber Gray was not a gunfighter. He could handle firearms well, better than most men, but as far as showdowns and quick draws were concerned, he simply was not cut from the right cloth. He had killed only three men in his forty plus years; two during the War and one purely out of necessity. Today he would be going up against a kid with a reputation and a fancy, low-slung gun. A kid who had gunned down twelve men in two years, if the stories were to be believed. A short instant from now either one or both of them would lay, gunshot and bleeding, on the saloon's sawdust floor. Timber could only pray that he would be the one left standing.

Ramsey had tied his mare to the hitching post and was approaching the saloon. Timber could hear the hollow drumming of his boots on the dirty boards of the sidewalk out front and the metallic clink of his fancy silver spurs. Timber glanced over at Sonny, then at the four gamblers. They all stared back at him, the tension in the air almost a living thing. Their eyes wished him luck, for they too had heard of Jess Ramsey. The wolfer turned his attention back to the bar mirror lined with liquor bottles. He laid his hand on the walnut handle of his short-barreled Colt.

The door opened and the kid came in. He was about to close it, when he noticed the man standing at the bar. Jess stared hard at the wolfer's back, suddenly recognizing the worn sheepskin coat and the silverbelly hat. A thin grin creased his lean face, but beyond the smile was a trace of nervousness.

He shifted the tail of his duster aside and slipped the thong off his pistol without giving it a second thought.

"Timber Gray!" he called out sharply, drawing the fancy silver .45 from its studded holster.

The wolf hunter turned and fired his own revolver. He was surprised to see the boy's gun out and belching flame. *So the tales are true,* thought Gray amid the noise and smoke. *He is fast and I'm dead.*

But that was not the case. The bullet from Ramsey's gun missed Timber by inches, splintering wood and cutting a long groove across the mahogany bartop. However, the wolfer's shot rang true. Crimson blossomed in the center of the kid's shirtfront as he stumbled backward. The fancy pistol flew from his fingers, knocking over a brass spittoon ten feet away.

The sulfurous pall of gunsmoke hung heavily in the room and, for a moment, the only sound heard was the fading echoes of the two shots. Timber Gray numbly holstered his gun and walked over to where the kid lay. Jess Ramsey had been dead before he hit the floor, killed by a perfect shot through the heart. His eyes stared dumbly up at his adversary, expressing a look of great bewilderment. At the moment of death his emotion had been one of utter disbelief, rather than fear.

"Well, I'll be damned," swore Sonny Dill. "I'd heard he was faster than that."

"Just goes to show you what a lot of wild stories usually add up to in the end," stated one of the poker players.

"Oh, he was fast, all right," Timber told them. "I was just lucky, that's all."

"I'd best fetch the sheriff," said Sonny. He shrugged on his coat and headed down the boardwalk toward the end of town.

Abruptly, two shots echoed from the direction of Doc Barrett's house. The first was the thunderous report of the Sharps breachloader. The second was that of a revolver. Timber Gray fetched his rifle from where it leaned beside the bar, stepped over the kid's dead body, and made his way onto the boarded walkway outside.

Avery Gimble was running down the street like Satan himself was prodding his rump with a pitchfork. The Sharps bellowed again and, this time, Gray spotted Luke Bell standing on the balcony of the house's upper floor. The shot blew the hat plumb off the bountyman's head, sending him scrambling down the street even faster.

Elijah Cox stepped out just as Gimble reached the general store. "Luke Bell is down at the doctor's place," Avery gasped, trying to catch his breath. "Me and Ted walked in on him. Ted drew his gun, but Bell shot him with that big rifle. I chased him upstairs, but that dadblamed sawbones went for his scattergun, so I came for you."

"I'll take care of it," Elijah said with a grin. He checked the loads in his ten gauge and closed the breach with a snap. "You go over to the saloon and fetch Jess. I heard some shooting a while ago, so he must be raising some hell over there."

Timber stepped back into the saloon before either man could see him. Avery Gimble started across the rutted street to the Cattleman, while Cox sauntered confidently up the walkway toward the doctor's home. The wolfer stepped behind the door, clutching the Winchester in both hands.

"Jess!" bellowed the big bounty hunter. "Get your skinny butt out here! Elijah need us over at the..."

Avery's words caught in his throat as he stepped up on the boardwalk and saw the kid's body lying there on the other side of the saloon doorway. He cursed softly, drew a Smith & Wesson .44 from his waistband, and stepped inside, ready to put lead to the one responsible.

Timber Gray wasn't about to chance another gunfight. The first thing through the door was the .44 fisted in Avery's big hand. The wolfer brought the barrel of his rifle down against the man's hairy wrist with a forceful crack. The gun spun from Gimble's hand and hit the floor with a thud. It went off with a roar, drilling a hole in a beer keg behind the bar.

"What in tarnation?" he growled, then stumbled back out the doorway as Timber swung his rifle around, splitting Gimble's nose with the buttplate. The bounty hunter's weight crashed through the hitching rail, splintering the heavy wooden beam. He landed hard in the street, lying on his back and shaking his head.

By the time Timber got out the door, Avery Gimble was already on his feet and fighting mad. The wolfer swung his rifle again, but Avery's massive paw caught it before it struck. He wrenched the repeater plumb out of Timber's hands and tossed it into the street.

"Now I've got you, wolf hunter!" growled Avery. His scarred face grew even uglier as he smiled in anticipation. "You're gonna wish you'd stayed up there in Montana when I get finished with you!"

The big man was much quicker and stronger than Timber had first judged. A ham-like fist lashed out, hitting Gray square in the teeth, while the other grabbed hold of his shirtfront. Avery lifted the hunter completely off his feet and slammed him into an awning post. The force shook ice and snow from the eaves and a small avalanche landed atop Gimble's head and shoulders. Timber was released, but the man shrugged off the snow and came for him again.

Timber laid a solid punch on Avery's jaw, following it with an uppercut to his already injured nose. The bountyman yelped in pain. The blow didn't seem to slow him down one bit. It just seemed to enrage him even more. He caught Timber in a crushing bearhug and lifted him into the air, tightening his brawny arms around the wolfer's ribcage. A dull ache slowly turned into suffocating agony and Timber knew he couldn't take much more. Using all the strength he could muster, he clapped his hands against Avery's ears. Avery staggered off the edge of the walkway, dropping his foe as he clutched at his ringing ears. Timber slumped to the dirty, churned snow of the street. His lungs heaved for air as fiery pain throbbed in his sides.

"You need some help with that polecat, Timber?" called Trampus Haines from the porch of the general store. He already had his shirtsleeves rolled halfway up his skinny forearms.

"No," rasped Timber hoarsely. He spat blood from a busted lip as Avery Gimble waded forward for another attack. "Let me end this on my own."

"I'm gonna kill you, Gray!" swore Avery. He reached down to grab the wolf hunter, but Timber struck first. His boot kicked out and hit the big man squarely in the gut. Avery doubled over with a husky grunt. Then Timber came in close and began slugging. Again and again, his punches landed on mark; bruising flesh, bringing blood, and driving the bounty hunter out into the center of Greybull's main street. Avery tried to land some blows of his own, but his big fists met nothing but air. After withstanding a dozen blows, the giant finally fell. His blood speckled the filthy slush of the street as he lay there beaten, unable and unwilling to finish the brawl he had started.

Timber himself looked and felt as if he'd been trampled by a stampede of Texas steers. He groaned as he stooped to pick up his hat and rifle, and figured he must have a couple of cracked ribs. He had gone up against a man twice his size and whipped him. Now all he had to worry about was the confrontation between Elijah Cox and Luke Bell.

Avery Gimble moaned feebly and attempted to get up. The toll of his injuries were too great, however, and he slumped back to the icy ground. "Keep an eye on this jackass for me, will you, Trampus?" asked Timber.

"I surely will," agreed Haines. He stood close by, his eyes on the big fellow and his hand near his holstered gun.

Timber Gray worked the lever of his Winchester and found it undamaged. He glanced up the street toward the end of town. There was still no sign of Sonny Dill and the sheriff. With cold determination set on his battered face, Timber started up the street toward the two-story clapboard house of J.W. Barrett.

Elijah Cox stood at the gate of the doctor's white picket fence. The ugly length of the sawed-off shotgun was resting on one narrow shoulder. He stood there, his gold-studded grin broad and easy-going, but his eyes as dark and calculating as that of a rattler.

Luke Bell leaned weakly against the railing of the upper balcony. His dark face was tired and sickly, but his expression was one of angry defiance. The cowhand held Gray's Sharps breachloader tightly, the forestock braced atop the ornate railing. The gaping muzzle yawned threateningly down at the grinning bountyman.

"I'm through running from you, Cox!" said Luke. "I've killed one of your boys already and I won't hesitate to put a bullet in you, too. Your best bet would be to get on your horse and light a shuck back to Colorado."

Elijah laughed harshly. "And give up that thousand dollar bounty? I've killed white men for much less than that. You've been a tough one to corner, I'll admit, but you ain't no Wild Bill Hickock. You're just a dumb cowboy with more gun than you can handle. I'll blow you clean off that porch before you can even fire that old buffalo gun."

"I wouldn't sell the man short if I was you, Cox," warned Timber from the double doors of Jones' livery. "He's as tough as a rawhide lariat and hellfire mean when he's riled."

Elijah was startled by the sound of Gray's voice. Perhaps he thought Jess or Avery had already taken care of the bearded wolfer back at the Cattleman Saloon. "You stay out of this, Gray!" he yelled over his shoulder. "After I'm through with Bell, it'll be your turn!"

"No!" proclaimed Luke. His sunken eyes flashed angrily down at the bounty hunter. "It ends right here and now. Just between you and me."

"That suits me just fine," said Cox. With a grin, he brought the ten gauge down off his shoulder and fired without warning.

Luke stumbled back as the first load hit the porch post, riddling it with buckshot. The cowhand dropped to the balcony floor as the scattergun's second barrel erupted in flame and burnt powder. An upstairs window caved inward under a hail of pellets, but none found their intended victim.

The cowboy rolled across the floor of the upstairs porch as wooden slivers and shards of glass rained down upon him. He brought the Sharps up, poked the octagon barrel through the slats of the railing, and fired.

Elijah Cox staggered back, momentarily stunned. The double-barreled shotgun slipped from his grasp and hit the snow at his feet. "Damn!' cursed the bounty hunter. He clamped a hand to the side of his head and the palm came away coated with blood. "My ear! You shot off my ear, you

163

confounded jigaboo!" Cox lost no time grieving over his loss. He drew both revolvers from his gunbelt and commenced to firing.

The .44 Dragoons boomed like twin cannons, chewing up the railing of the banister and the whitewashed wall that lay beyond. Luke scrambled to reload the Sharps. He dropped the block of the breach, inserted a fresh cartridge, and cocked the beefy hammer. When the final shots from Elijah's pistols rang out, the Negro got to his feet. He limped to the balcony railing and brought the Sharps solidly to his shoulder.

The bounty hunter's guns clicked on empty chambers. In sudden panic, he tossed them aside and went for the hideout gun he always kept concealed in the back of his waistband. But as he brought the little .41 derringer up to armslength, he knew he was too late. He saw the flash of burnt powder, heard the ear-splitting report, and felt the shearing pain of the fifty caliber bullet as it tunneled through his belly and out the small of his back.

Timber Gray watched as Cox collapsed to the snowy earth. He held the repeating rifle at his hip and moved in closer. The bounty hunter lay on his back, twitching in agony as his life ebbed away. Blood ran in rivulets from his fatal wound and Elijah's ugly face was as pale as fine porcelain.

Luke limped from the front door and stood near the steps. "Is he dead?"

"He's hanging on," Timber told him. "But not for very long. No man can take a fifty-caliber slug in the gut and live to brag to his grandchildren about it."

They both looked around as Sheriff Henry King hurried up the street with Sonny Dill following close behind. "I heard the shots clear over at the jail. What happened here?"

"A couple of lowdown bounty hunters came to my office and tried to kill Bell here," explained Doc Barrett, still toting his twelve gauge. "Then this fellow showed up and started shooting up the place like a madman."

Elijah Cox lifted a shaky hand and pointed an accusing finger at the black cowpoke. "That man's wanted for the murder of Daniel Spencer of Durango, Colorado." He fumbled the crumpled wanted poster from his coat pocket and handed it to the lawman.

Sheriff King unfolded the broadsheet and studied it carefully. He glanced over at the injured Negro. "Are you Luke Bell?"

Luke swallowed dryly and nodded in sullen agreement.

"Yeah, and he's worth a thousand in gold," said Cox. Even as death approached, Elijah's dark eyes sparkled with greed.

King looked down at the bounty hunter and shook his head in disgust. "You dadblamed fool. Got yourself gutshot on account of a worthless piece of paper." He wadded the poster into a ball and tossed it to the ground.

"What do you mean... worthless?" muttered Elijah.

"Bell here is innocent," the sheriff told him. "Every lawman in the territory has known that for nearly two weeks now. Seems that some Mexican cardsharp got drunk and talking down in San Luis right after the mayor was killed. He got to bragging about putting a bullet to a gringo mayor and taking his gold. A U.S. Marshal named Farnsworth overheard his boasting and took him back to Durango for trial. I heard that Mex was hung in the town square Sunday before last."

"Then Luke is free and clear," pointed out Timber.

"He most certainly is."

Elijah's face twisted into a mixture of agony and rage. "Why, you lousy son of a..." He started to lift his derringer, but a violent fit of coughing seized him. A bloody froth ran over his bristled chin and he collapsed... dead.

Luke hobbled over and stared down bitterly at the man who had hounded him for the better part of a month. "I killed him because he gave me no other choice," he told the sheriff.

"I ain't about to pin that on you, Bell," assured King. "Cox was a mean and dangerous man. I figure he brought it on himself."

As the crowd of curious townfolk dispersed, Doc Barrett took Luke's elbow and steered him back toward the house. "I've still got to finish dressing that wound of yours. And, after that, you need a hot meal and rest. A good, long rest."

"I ain't gonna argue with you none," said Luke with genuine gratitude.

Timber turned to see Trampus standing nearby. "Where's Avery Gimble?" he asked.

"When he heard that Cox was shot, he jumped on Ramsey's hoss and hightailed it back to Colorado. Turned out he was the stinking polecat I figured him to be. Didn't even stick around long enough to give his friends a decent burial."

The wolfer clapped a hand on Haines' shoulder and smiled. "How's about joining me for a drink," he offered as they started back down the boarded walkway of Greybull's southern side. "I seem to recollect I've got a bottle waiting for me back at the Cattleman Saloon."

"I believe I'll take you up on that," said Trampus. As they made their way to the drinking establishment, the storekeeper regarded his friend with a broad grin. Things had been downright drab and depressing there in Greybull, until Timber Gray had showed up and changed it for them all. Whether he actually knew it or not, the wolf hunter had broken through their day-to-day drudgery and brought the spirit of the wild frontier back to them, if only for a short time.

Chapter Twenty-Three

Timber Gray rode into the Bighorn Mountains for the last time that winter.

He took his slate gray roan and the two Missouri mules up the snowy passes and along the rocky ridges of Cloud Peak. Again, as had happened recently, uneasiness pressed on the wolfer's mind. His stay in Greybull had changed him. It had eased his loneliness and lifted his spirit from the grave of his unfortunate past. Timber felt halfway torn between civilization and wilderness. He longed for the remote isolation of the lofty mountains, yet his thoughts kept returning to Trampus and the townspeople of Greybull. And, still, he found himself thinking of Lenora Cook and her young'uns. They were disturbing thoughts, having to do with family and home. And that was two things that Timber Gray had not seriously considered since crossing the Mississippi River and striking westward.

A day's ride took him up the winding pass to the junction at Mountain Cross. Snow packed the crossed canyons. If any of the six remaining wolves had perished beneath the crushing weight of the snowslide, that would be that many pelts the wolf hunter would be cheated of. But Timber somehow knew that—like Elijah Cox and his men—Cripplefoot and his pack had narrowly escaped the impact of the avalanche. Going back down the pass a few hundred yards, Timber found an alternate route that took him further up the sloping pinnacle of the Bighorn's rocky face.

He reached the hidden pocket of Wolf Gorge before nightfall. As he had feared, the wolves had come and gone. The dall sheep still hung from the twisted limb of the oak, but its torso was stripped of hide and meat. Cripplefoot and his followers had feasted well before moving onward to the southern-most peaks of the mountain range.

For the next few days, Timber pursued his prey, finding their trail and then losing it a mile or so later. Cripplefoot was a crafty devil; an animal who sometimes moved more like a ghost than a common wolf. He went out of his way to conceal his tracks. The other five, while not nearly as shrewd as their leader, did their best to follow his example.

The thing that Timber feared most was losing them to the vast wilderness ahead. The further south they traveled, the greater the chance of escape. Already the towering peaks and cavernous passes were giving way to wooded foothills. Soon the Bighorn range would flatten out and turn into open plains. The Powder River Valley stretched southward for nearly a hundred miles. Timber knew if the pack reached the sprawling grasslands, they would be out of his grasp for good.

Only the burning desire for Old Cripplefoot's hide kept the wolfer from turning back. Many times before, he had stalked the white wolf, and many times he had lost him, as had countless trappers and hunters over the last forty years. It wasn't bagging an even pack of fifty murderous wolves that mattered now. It was Old Cripplefoot. He was the only prize that would settle the longest hunt of Timber Gray's career.

The days drew on, growing colder and gloomier as January ended and February began. Snow began to fall regularly, covering the rocky slopes and making the way treacherous for Timber and his horses. Slowly, his supplies began to dwindle. Soon all he would have to keep himself alive would be the two rifles and the limited supply of cartridges in his pack. But, then, the seasoned hunter had survived on less than that before, and under much worse conditions.

The confrontation came to a head on the third day of the new month. Timber Gray awoke to find fresh tracks no more than ten feet from the smoldering ashes of his campfire. The closest tracks—and the boldest of the six—were the mismatched prints of Old Cripplefoot. Forgetting breakfast, Timber saddled the roan, readied the mules, and headed out in the direction of the wolf tracks. They led plainly along a narrow pass; one that grew steeper and more closed in as he rode onward. It finally ended in a box canyon. The dead-end gorge was a natural trap if ever he had seen one and Timber knew that he had ridden blindly into its jaws.

There, at the far end of the canyon, stood five of the remaining pack; two she-wolves and three full-grown males. They were powerfully built and perfect examples of the timber wolf breed. Standing in a widening arch, twenty feet between each one, they snapped and growled, their silvery eyes cold and intense, trying to shake his nerve.

Gray slipped the hitch knot off his saddle and secured the pack mules to the branches of a scraggly pine. He walked his horse further into the box canyon. His eyes moved from one wolf to the next, searching out the one he sought. Even though Cripplefoot was not among them, Timber could sense his presence. The Ghost Wolf was somewhere close by; watching, observing, testing what he was truly made of.

"I hope you're ready for this, old hoss," he whispered to the charcoal roan. "Cause I ain't exactly sure I am." The horse twitched its ears and snorted loudly at the strong scent of meat-eating scavengers. But the sound was not out of nervousness, but anticipation. Timber Gray had known of such animals before. He had encountered many during the War Between the States. Born of noble breed and a bold heart, the gray roan was a fighting horse; a sturdy steed that would gallop to the charge and would not spook at the brittle crack of gunfire or the throaty snarl of wild beasts.

The wolves watched him suspiciously as he rode to the center of the rocky canyon floor, closing the distance between them until only a hundred yards remained. Timber slowly reached down to the sides of his saddle. Shucking both the Winchester and the Sharps from their sheaths, he cocked the hammers and spurred the horse into action.

The beasts lunged forward as he did. Their muscles flowed like quicksilver and their powerful jaws snapped and strained, eager to rend flesh and spill warm red blood. Timber braced the Sharps against his hip and squeezed the trigger. A thunderous boom split the canyon air. The heavy- grain slug caught the largest male wolf directly in the brisket, drilling him from bow to stern. His fur matted with blood, the animal spun in mid-leap and rolled thirty feet before landing in a motionless heap on the canyon floor.

Onward the roan charged. Timber returned the smoking buffalo gun to its boot. He lifted the repeater to his shoulder and swept its sights past the horse's bobbing head. Two wolves veered toward him, intending to hamstring the horse and bring it down. Timber began to fire in rapid succession, working the lever as fast as he could manage. One of the beasts fell to the hail of bullets, its winter coat erupting in six bloody patches. However, the other kept on coming, despite the slugs buried in its torso and limbs. The wolfer fired until the wolf disappeared from view, darting at the legs of the gray roan. Timber thought he had failed to save the roan, but the spirited horse came through. It bucked angrily and struck out with flashing hooves. The wolf dropped in its tracks, its skull cleaved in half by the mount's unbridled fury.

The bearded rider surged forward to confront the remaining two. A she-wolf ran straight for them. Right when the wolf moved in, intent on stripping flesh from the roan's nimble legs, the horse sprang, leaping completely over the snarling animal. Timber twisted in the saddle, drew his .45, and fired. The revolver's slug caught the beast neatly in the base of the skull, bringing death instantaneously.

Timber Gray was turning to confront the last of the five, when he was knocked forcefully from the saddle. He caught a quick glimpse of fur and flashing fangs, before he hit the frozen earth with bone-jarring impact. The wolf rolled over him as they fell, but was on its feet again and after him before he could regain his senses. His hands were empty. The revolver and the lever-action had fallen from his grasp when he hit the ground.

The wolf was suddenly upon him, ripping, tearing into him with savage fervor. Timber kicked and lashed out, but his hands came back gashed and torn, streaming with his own blood. When the cold grip of panic finally began to overtake the hunter, his attacker made its first—and last—mistake. Its slaverous jaws clamped down viciously on Gray's forearm, sending a lance of pain coursing through the hunter's limb and unleashing memories of a similar attack fifteen long years ago.

Thoughts of Chestnut Creek washed over him and he lost all control. For one horrible moment, Timber was back in the mountains of eastern Tennessee. He could feel the cool water of the stream sweeping around him as a rabid wolf tore into his flailing arm, infecting him with the germ of the mind-burning

171

madness. Timber pushed the tormenting past aside and confronted the present. A fiery rage engulfed him; a rage sparked of hatred and loathing for the timber-bred beast.

"I'll not let it happen again, you filthy devil!" vowed Timber Gray. He drew the skinning knife from under his coat. "Not ever again!"

He plunged the knife's honed blade under the wolf's ribs with a savagery of his very own. The animal yelped and attempted to escape. But the hunter was not through with the beast. Again and again he jabbed, slashing and gutting. When Timber finally came to his senses, the beast lay on the snowy earth, limp and lifeless.

The hunter slipped his knife back into its sheath. Shakily, he got to his feet, grimacing in sudden pain. The bruised ribs from his brawl with Avery Gimble ached dully in his left side and his hands and forearm burned, bleeding slowly from the wolf's near fatal attack. He found his Colt and returned it to its holster. The Winchester was beyond use now, the barrel bent at an awkward angle from its fall to the rocky earth.

Timber stumbled toward his horse. The battle with the five wolves had exhausted him, and the aches and pains hadn't helped matters any. He reached the horse, wrapping a sore hand around the saddlehorn to steady himself. His blue-gray eyes flashed with heated anger as he pulled the big Sharps from its boot.

"Cripplefoot!" he bellowed. His voice bounced off the steep canyon walls of jagged shale, followed by the crisp snap of metal as he inserted a fresh round into the rifle's breach and closed the block. "I know you're around here somewhere, so you'd best show yourself and get it over with!"

Silence mocked him as he waited. He stood there, alert and on his guard, the .50 rifle held expectantly in his bloody hands. Only the lonely moan of the winter wind pressed on his ears, as well as the nervous shifting of the roan's hooves. Then a clatter of stones rolling down the steep face of the canyon wall sounded directly behind him. He whirled, lifting his eyes to the source of the noise. A crooked grin crossed his bearded face. It was the ugly grin of a man nearly consumed by hate.

There, standing nobly atop the far wall of the box canyon, was the magnificent white wolf of the Rockies. The beast men called Old Cripplefoot.

"I've finally got you, you mangy scoundrel!" rasped the wolfer. Smoothly, he set the Sharps' curved buttplate against his shoulder, thumbed back the hammer, and lifted the heavy barrel skyward.

Timber Gray laughed in triumph, his eyes almost crazed in their excitement. The sights wavered, then settled squarely on the wolf's downy breastbone. He laid his finger gently on the trigger and prepared to squeeze. But something stopped him. He shifted his gaze from Cripplefoot's silvery chest to his massive pointed face. The old wolf's dark eyes were locked unerringly on the hunter's own.

Timber knew he had him. He had only to pull the trigger to claim the ultimate prize of his long hunt. But his muscles remained frozen, as if time itself had been halted by the hand of God. He realized then that this was the closest he had ever been to the great white wolf. No more than twenty yards stretched between the hunter and his prey and, suddenly, starkly, he saw the animal for what it truly was.

Cripplefoot was a flea-bitten shell of a wolf compared to the legend that had surrounded him for the past forty years. The animal's white coat was patchy and streaked with age. Countless scars etched his hide, placed there by the glancing shots of a hundred mountain hunters. Timber was sure there were bullets still in the old wolf, as well as an arrowhead or two lodged beneath the skin. Cripplefoot's right hindquarter bulged misshapenly, as if he had broken his hip years before and it had healed improperly.

The wolf was not the ruthless, bloodthirsty beast that so many had made him out to be. No, Old Cripplefoot was just a poor shadow of the legend that had swept the Great Divide since the days of mountain man rendezvous and beaver trapping in the Yellowstone. He was just an old Methuselah of a timber wolf who appeared to be near his end, having survived the last great hunt of his existence.

Fifteen long years of wolf-hating burnt out right then and there. Timber Gray felt the emotion fizzle and die in the pit of his soul like a lit fuse with nothing to set off. He stared blankly at the wolf's face, searching for some trace of malice that might rekindle the hatred, but there was none. Cripplefoot's narrow countenance showed only a weary peace.

"Aw, hell!" said the hunter. He shifted his sights a fraction and fired. The big 50-caliber slug hit the cliff beneath the wolf's feet, sending sharp fragments of shale spinning into the cold air of early February. Cripplefoot did not move a muscle. He stood his ground and continued to stare his pursuer down.

Timber let his buffalo gun sag until it hung heavily in his hands. "I reckon we're alot alike, old fella," the man said with a sigh. "Excepting maybe I've got a few more years on me. And it sure would be a shame to waste them alone in these mountains with nothing better to do than hunt critters for a few dollars bounty."

There seemed to be an expression of agreement in Cripplefoot's ancient eyes. Perhaps the wolf knew the kind of life Gray had led, for he too had lived through similar times. For the most part, he had ignored his own kind and wandered the mountains and prairies in search of something that all creatures, man or beast, hoped to someday attain. A healing of the wounded soul or, simply, peace of mind.

174

Standing there in that lonely dead-end canyon, Timber Gray knew that both of them had finally reached that goal… and had paid a bitter price in getting there.

"Go on now and git," Timber called up to him. "Before I change my mind."

The white wolf remained on the ledge for a final moment, then turned and disappeared. The sound of his leaving lingered in Timber's ears and then gradually faded into silence. The hunter's eyes remained fixed on the lip of the shale wall for a long time, for he knew that he would never see Old Cripplefoot or the likes of him ever again.

Turning back to the wolves that laid around the canyon floor, he set to the unpleasant task of skinning and preparing the hides for the trip back to Greybull. The end of a hunt had always been a cause for celebration for the man called Timber Gray. But this time there was much more to look forward to. He had discovered a fresh trail in life, one that would hopefully be less rocky and less lonely than the one he had journeyed for so very long.

Chapter Twenty-Four

Evening was descending on the town of Greybull, Wyoming when Timber Gray climbed down out of his saddle and tethered his horse to the hitching rail outside the general store. Taking his skinning knife, he cut the wolf pelts off the pack mule. The warm glow of a kerosene lamp welcomed him as he slung the bundle of hides over his shoulder and opened the door of Haines Mercantile.

Trampus wasn't there, but someone was busy behind the counter, stocking the shelves. Surprisingly enough, it turned out to be Luke Bell who glanced up at the hollow jangle of a cow bell over the door. Luke looked to be in good health and high spirits, decked out in a white shirt, bowtie, and clerk's apron.

"What's an ornery cowpoke like you doing here?" Timber asked, shaking the black man's hand.

"I decided to take up a new line of work," Luke told him. He found his walking cane and limped from behind the store counter. "Had me a little money left over from last summer's drive, so I bought into Trampus's store as a partner. Thought it was about time to stick to one spot for a change. Time to settle down."

"I know exactly what you mean, Luke," said Timber. He took his tobacco pouch from his shirt pocket and rolled himself a cigarette. "What about the cattle business? Won't you miss it none?"

"I suppose I will. But now I've got me something rock steady. Good neighbors, respectability, and some solid roots to put down; things mighty rare for a man of my race. Anyhow, no decent cattleman would have need of a crippled cowhand on his payroll."

Timber followed the new storekeeper back into the stockroom. Luke unlocked and unbolted the pantry, where the other wolf skins laid in a side bin. The hunter tossed the remaining five on the heap. They would stay under lock and key until it was time for Timber to saddle up and head north for Miles City.

"Where's Trampus this evening?" asked the hunter.

"He's over at the stage office," Luke replied, slipping the skeleton key back into his shirt pocket. "The evening stage just came in a while ago and he went over to pick up the mail."

"I've got business over yonder myself." Timber slipped his hat back on and stepped into the cold twilight of the February dusk. With a deep breath, he crossed the street to the Central Overland. He had given some things serious thought coming down off the mountain and knew that he would have to take the first step if he was to make a fresh start.

"Timber!" greeted Trampus as the wolfer shook off the cold and stepped inside the stage office. "How'd you make out up on the Bighorn? Did those dadblamed wolves get a taste of your lead?"

Timber nodded. "All except one."

Haines' smile turned into a sour frown. "Old Cripplefoot?"

"The one and only."

The storekeeper shook his head in bewilderment. "I told you that wolf was bad medicine. Just a wailing wisp of a ghost, that's all there is to him."

Timber stepped over to the counter where Cecil Thurman, the stage clerk, stood. "Is that telegraph up to sending a couple of messages?" asked the hunter.

"The lines were iced over last week, but the weather's warmed up a mite since then. It should be in good working order by now." He took a pencil from behind his ear and poised it over a pad of lined paper.

"Both of these go to Miles City. The first wire goes to Louis B. Whittaker. Write it: LOU… GOT FORTY-NINE OF THE FIFTY. WILL BRING THE HIDES TO YOU IN THE NEXT WEEK. HAVE MY BOUNTY READY, AS WELL AS A GOOD STIFF SHOT OF THAT FANCY FRENCH LIQUOR. And sign that TIMBER GRAY."

Cecil nodded, jotting down the words to be sent. "And the other one?"

Timber felt all hot under the collar and nervous. "Make the second one out to Lenora Cook in care of the Demorest Hotel." The hunter hesitated, then went on. "Word it: LENORA… WOULD LIKE TO TRY FOR THAT BETTER LIFE, IF YOU FEEL THE SAME WAY. WILL BE IN TOWN SOON FOR YOUR ANSWER. You can sign that one JEFFERSON GRAY."

Trampus gaped, his jaw nearly dropping to his shirtfront. "Now, don't tell me the old loner is finally getting hitched and settling down!"

"I'm hoping to if she'll have me," Timber answered, his face reddening in embarrassment. "Besides, I reckon it's about time for me to stop running wild and start living again."

"I'm right proud for you," said Trampus, pounding his old friend on the back. "How's about coming over to the house and sitting down to supper with us. Myrtle Belle is fixing fried chicken tonight."

"Sounds mighty tempting," Gray admitted. "But tonight I'm not much in the mood for company. I've got me some thinking to do before I leave for Montana in the morning. Gotta put some things straight in my mind, like where I've been and where I'm going."

"I understand and don't blame you," said Trampus. "But you're certainly welcome to breakfast tomorrow morning. How does eggs and smoked ham sound to you?"

Timber shook his friend's hand warmly. "Just so Myrtle Belle cooks up a passel of her homemade biscuits to go with them," he said with a smile. Then the two parted company; Haines heading back to the store and Gray walking in the direction of the Cattleman Saloon.

It was a Friday night and the place was packed with men, drinking and smoking and losing their hard-earned pay at poker. Timber Gray stepped up to the bar and caught Sonny Dill's eye from where he poured a drink at the end of the counter. "What'll it be, Timber?" he asked.

"A bottle of your best sipping whiskey and a glass."

The bartender set a bottle and shotglass before him. "Anything else?"

"Just a corner table to sit at till closing time." The hunter paid the barkeep, took his bottle, and found himself an empty table near the back wall.

Timber settled down in a creaky hardwood chair and poured his first shot. He paid no one any mind, until two hard-looking characters left the bar and ambled his way. Soon they stood before his table, beer mugs in their hands.

"Would you be Timber Gray?" asked the taller man.

"Yes." He eyed the two suspiciously. "Why?"

"We heard you went after Old Cripplefoot and lost him," said the other, a squat man with a wiry growth of rusty red beard.

Men had brought his failures to light before and their joking has usually ended in fistfights sparked out of anger and bitterness. Timber didn't know if the motive of these fellows was the same as all the others. If they intended to taunt the old wolfer into another barroom brawl, they would walk away disappointed that night. Timber Gray would not be enraged by their laughter any longer. No, all he wanted to do was drink his whiskey and be left alone.

"Yes, I lost him again," said Timber. He lifted his eyes to the pair. "What of it?"

"We'd just like to sit and hear your story." The lanky fellow smiled, his face friendly enough. "Me and Rusty here, we tracked the critter for nearly two years, but never had no luck with him. I got me a perfect shot at him once and, heaven help me, I swear I got him clean through the heart! But he was gone when we got to the ledge he was standing on. Just a few specks of blood on the ground and nothing more."

The two hunters stood there expectantly for a long moment. Then Timber laughed and poured himself another drink. "Pull up a chair, boys, and sit a spell."

The remainder of the night would be spent drinking and swapping tales of the Ghost Wolf. On about closing time, when the chairs were set upon the tables and Sonny was wiping down the bar for the night, they would hear the banshee howl of a lone wolf drift from the distant peaks of the Bighorn Mountains.

And they would trade a mutual smile of grudging admiration and toast Old Cripplefoot, the only wolf who had escaped the vengeful gun of Timber Gray.

About the Author

Ronald Kelly was born November 20, 1959, in Nashville, Tennessee, where he was raised a Southern Baptist. He attended Pegram Elementary School and Cheatham County Central High School (both in Ashland City, Tennessee) before starting his writing career.

Ronald Kelly began his writing career in 1986 and quickly sold his first short story, "Breakfast Serial," to *Terror Time Again* magazine. His first novel, *Hindsight* was released by Zebra Books in 1990. His audiobook collection, *Dark Dixie: Tales of Southern Horror*, was on the nominating ballot of the 1992 Grammy Awards for Best Spoken Word or Non-Musical Album. Zebra published seven of Ronald Kelly's novels from 1990 to 1996. Ronald's short fiction work has been published by *Cemetery Dance*, *Borderlands 3*, *Deathrealm*, *Dark at Heart*, *Hot Blood: Seeds of Fear*, and many more. After selling hundreds of thousands of books, the bottom dropped out of the horror market in 1996. So, when Zebra dropped their horror line in October 1996, Ronald Kelly stopped writing for almost ten years and worked various jobs including welder, factory worker, production manager, drugstore manager, and custodian.

In 2006, Ronald Kelly started writing again. Since then, he has written and published several new novels (*Hell Hollow*, *Restless Shadows*, and *The Buzzard Zone*), numerous short story collections, and has become an elder statesman of Southern-Fried Horror in his chosen genre. In 2021, his collection of extreme horror tales, *The Essential Sick Stuff*, won the Splatterpunk Award for Best Collection. He is currently working on The Saga of Dead-Eye, a five-volume horror western series. Book One, *Vampires, Zombies, & Mojo Men* was recently published by Thunderstorm Books.

Ronald Kelly currently lives in a backwoods hollow in Brush Creek, Tennessee, with his wife and young'uns.

Book List

Novels
Blood Kin
Father's Little Helper (re-released as Twelve Gauge)
Fear
Fear Eternal (forthcoming)
Hell Hollow
Hindsight
Moon of the Werewolf (re-released as Undertaker's Moon)
Pitfall
Restless Shadows
Something Out There (re-released as The Dark'Un)
The Buzzard Zone
The China Doll
The Possession (re-released as Burnt Magnolia)
The Saga of Dead-Eye, Book One: Vampires, Zombies, & Mojo Men
The Saga of Dead-Eye, Book Two: Werewolves, Swamp Critters, & Hellacious Haints
The Saga of Dead-Eye, Book Three: Man-Eaters, Mummies, & Murderous Maniacs
Timber Gray

Novellas
Flesh Welder

Collections
After the Burn
Cumberland Furnace and Other Fear Forged Fables
Dark Dixie

Dark Dixie II

Haunt of Southern-Fried Fear

Irish Gothic: Tales of Celtic Horror

Long Chills

Midnight Tide & Other Seaside Stories

Mister Glow-Bones & Other Halloween Tales

More Sick Stuff

Season's Creepings: Tales of Holiday Horror

Tales from the Southern-Fried Crypt

The Essential Sick Stuff

The Halloween Store and Other Tales of All Hallows' Eve

The Shrouded Tome: Ten Forgotten Fables

The Sick Stuff

The Web of La Sanguinaire and Other Arachnid Horrors

Twilight Hankerings

Unhinged

Vault of Southern-Fried Horror

Curious about other Crossroad Press books? Stop by our
website: http://crossroadpress.com
We offer quality writing
in digital, audio, and print formats.

Subscribe to our newsletter on the website homepage and
receive a free eBook.

www.ingramcontent.com/pod-product-compliance
Lightning Source LLC
Chambersburg PA
CBHW020637180626
46816CB00003B/1015